MEAT SANDWICHES

MEAT SANDWICHES

MORE ADVENTURES IN ABSURDITY

M. P. MACDOUGALL

Meat Sandwiches

MORE Adventures in Absurdity

M.P. MacDougall

DYSFUNCTIONAL DOZEN PRESS

ISBN: 978-1-962138-13-0

Cover design by M.P. MacDougall

This story is dedicated to my many family members and friends, whose strange Doppelgängers populate these stories.

Thanks for the inspiration and a lifetime of laughs.

1

THE ATTACK BADGER

Duke charged into the kitchen, grinning happily. "Lookit, man, lookit what my girlfriend's dad gave me!" He plunked a ratty-looking animal in the middle of the dining table, scattering utensils and dishes everywhere.

"AAGGHH!" Waylon yelped and fell over backwards in his chair. "What the heck is that thing?!?"

"It's a stuffed badger!" Duke said, laughing as Waylon picked himself up off the floor. "I'm gonna use it to freak people out!"

"I think it's working," I said. "Get it away from my scrambled eggs before it starts shedding."

"What should I name it?" Duke was ignoring me.

Waylon glared at him. "How about stupid son-of-a..."

"I don't care what you name it," I said as I snatched my eggs away from the moth-eaten thing. "As long as you keep it offa my plate."

The badger had been preserved in mid-lunge, teeth bared in a ferocious snarl. Its fur had worn thin in several places, giving it a subtle air of decay. It had one foreleg outstretched, but the paw had broken off at the wrist some decades earlier. All that remained was a couple of rusty wires protruding from its forearm. The result was a sort of cyborg-badger-fleabag effect. The thing was nasty, and Duke loved it.

———

DUKE, WAYLON AND I HAD BEEN FRIENDS SINCE HIGH SCHOOL. NOW OUT of school, we were splitting rent three ways in a large house. It was a decent arrangement, but not without its little annoyances - many of them caused by Duke's irritating behavior. He had a habit of cutting up his eggs at breakfast by madly slashing at them with his fork and knife at the same time, making an unholy racket and shaking the table so hard that Waylon's coffee would usually spill.

Waylon was a gentle giant who was slow to anger - he'd grab his cup and glare daggers across the table at Duke, but wouldn't say anything. Duke would happily grin and rock back and forth as he slashed his eggs into submission, oblivious that he was disturbing anything.

Another annoying habit was Duke's tendency to badly mispronounce words, titles or names, and then be impervious to correction. He once told me about a clock radio he wanted. "It's a Sound Sign," he said.

"Do you mean Soundesign?" I asked.

"That's what I said. Sound Sign."

"I think it's pronounced Sound - Design," I said.

"Yeah. Just like I said. Sound Sign."

I gritted my teeth. "Say it with me: Sound... Design..."

"What are you, deaf? That's what I said! Sound Sign."

He was also prone to singing along - loudly - with any music we happened to be playing. He'd sing so loudly that we couldn't hear the real music, and we'd end up leaving the room in frustration. Then Duke would put on his own favorite, which for several months straight was the nasally Hank Williams, Jr., song *"A Country Boy Can Survive."* Duke would greatly exaggerate the pronunciation, wailing "A CAHNTRY BOY KIN SURVAA-AAHVE!!" at the top of his lungs. I noticed a crack in one of our living room windows one day, and I was sure it was from his tone deaf caterwauling.

Duke was also not very modest. He'd get out of the shower, then get an uncontrollable urge to get something from the kitchen - before he got dressed. Many times, Waylon and I had our appetites killed when Duke came striding naked into the kitchen, opened the fridge and bent over to root around in the lower shelves. I took to eating my meals in my bedroom, but Waylon suffered on in quiet, simmering frustration. The badger was really not that unusual as far as Duke was concerned, but it added to the list of things that were slowly driving Waylon nuts.

"Isn't it cool?" Duke was saying. He picked the badger up and thrust it at me. "ARRR! RAHHRRR!!" I glanced across at Waylon. His facial tic was getting more pronounced by the minute.

"Yeah, Duke," I said, getting up. "It's great. I'm late for work."

"Me too," Waylon got up too, then slammed his dishes down on the counter. "Your turn to do dishes," he told Duke as he stomped out.

"RAHHHRRR!!!" Duke waved the badger at us on our way past.

As I backed my car out of the driveway, I could see the badger peeking around the edge of the living room window at me. Then Duke stuck his arm into view and the inanimate badger promptly attacked it, dragging Duke the rest of the way into view. By the time I drove off, Duke had the badger at his throat, pretending he was being eaten.

Moron.

THAT AFTERNOON, I GOT HOME BEFORE THE OTHERS. I WENT TO MY ROOM to put my things away, and couldn't help jumping in alarm when I found the badger comfortably resting on my pillow, tucked snug under my blankets with its curled lips and rusty paw jutting out. I ground my teeth and punted the thing out into the living room. Several minutes later, Duke came home.

"Didja find something in your bed?" he asked, leering at me and stifling a giggle.

"Yeah, yeah," I said. "Really funny."

"This thing is gonna be awesome," Duke said, picking up the badger and shoving it at me again. "RAHHRR! Just think how many people we can scare with it! It'll be great!"

"Great for you, maybe."

He glanced out the window as Waylon's truck rolled into the driveway. "Hey," he whispered. "Watch this!" He hustled over and placed the badger just inside the front door, poised like it was ready to pounce on intruders. I thought about warning Waylon, but morbid curiosity got the better of me. I watched, fascinated as Waylon stepped on the porch and opened the door. He had his foot halfway inside when he looked down and noticed the badger three inches from his ankle.

"AAAAIIIGGHH!!!" Waylon screamed like a twelve year old girl, staggered backward and fell off the porch into a bush. "SONOFA!!! I'm gonna kill you, you moron!!"

Duke was rolling around on the floor, holding his sides. "BWAHA-HA!! I got you, man! I got you!" He picked up the badger and thrust it out the door. "RAAHHHR!! Oh, you shoulda seen the look on your face!"

"You won't want to see the look on *your* face when I get finished with it," Waylon muttered. Then he saw me in the living room, biting back a laugh. "Were you in on this, too?"

"I'm an innocent bystander," I protested. "But I hafta admit, that was pretty funny. I didn't realize you could sing falsetto."

"Stupid badger," Waylon said. "Scared the crap outta me." He looked at Duke. "Laugh it up, funny boy. Payback's comin'."

Duke must not have heard him, because over the next few weeks, he had the badger greet Waylon at the door at least every other day. Waylon never got used to it - he'd end up shrieking in the bush next to the porch, or he'd drop whatever he was carrying and jump up and down in a panic. His nerves were getting thin.

THE LAST STRAW CAME ONE SATURDAY WHEN WE ALL DECIDED TO GO TO A swimming hole about twenty miles outside of town. There were some rock cliffs next to the river that were perfect for jumping off of, and since the temperatures had been near 100 all week, we were all eager to cool off. As we finished loading Waylon's truck for the ride to the river, Duke suddenly turned back to the house.

"Where you going?" Waylon asked. "We're leaving!"

"I forgot something," Duke said. "Hang on a sec!" He disappeared inside.

"If he brings that stupid badger, I'm gonna throw both of 'em off the cliff," Waylon said under his breath.

Duke emerged from the house with a gym bag under his arm. "Almost forgot my towel! Let's go!" He jumped in the back seat and settled in, grinning.

I shrugged at Waylon and climbed in the passenger side. Waylon got in and steered the truck out into the street. Duke immediately started singing along to the radio. Hillbilly rock band Lynyrd Skynyrd was on, singing *Sweet Home Alabama*, only Duke was changing the chorus to 'Sweet Home Oregon-a' and butchering the melody badly. Waylon and I ground our teeth in stereo.

Once we were on the highway outside of town, Duke stopped his wailing and leaned forward between the front seats. "Hey Waylon," he said. "Check it out."

Waylon and I turned at the same time. The badger was sitting on the console between the seats, snarling toward the dashboard like a rabid dog out for a ride, its rusty-wire paw raised in a gruesome salute.

"SONOFA!!!" Waylon almost drove the truck into a ditch while I screamed like a twelve year old girl.

Duke was in hysterics. "I got you both, man, I got you both!!"

I looked at Waylon. "You throw Duke, I'll throw the badger."

"Fair enough," Waylon said.

"Throw us where?" Duke asked.

We ignored him.

WHEN WE FINALLY GOT TO THE RIVER, DUKE SEEMED TO REALIZE THAT HE'D gone too far. "I'm sorry about the badger, Waylon," he said. "I probably shoulda left it at home. Whaddaya say we let bi-cons be bi-cons and forget about it?"

"You mean 'bygones'," I said.

"What?"

"Bygones. You mean, 'let bygones be bygones', not bi-cons. There's no such thing as a bi-con, anyway."

"That's what I said," Duke gave me a blank look. "Bi-cons."

"Bygones," I repeated.

"Yeah, bi-cons. Just like I said."

"BYGONES!! With a 'G'!!" I could feel my own facial tic developing.

Duke looked at me. "That's what I'm trying to tell you. Bi-cons."

I looked at Waylon. "Can we keep the badger, and get rid of him?"

"That's a good one, dude!" Duke slapped me on the back so hard I almost swallowed my tongue. "Let's go SWIMMIN'!" He bolted off down the trail to the cliff top.

"Maybe he'll hit his head on a rock and come up normal," Waylon said.

"Fat chance. Come on. I'm gonna go swimming, even if that means I have to be Duke's bi-con."

We spent the next several hours jumping off the rocks, swimming in the river and lounging in the sun. We forgot all about the badger. Then Waylon stood up.

"Where ya going?" I asked.

"Bathroom," he said, walking back up the trail into the trees. He was barely out of earshot before Duke started giggling.

I looked at him. "What did you do?"

Waylon's scream echoed through the trees and washed over us like a sonic boom. It reverberated off the campground on the opposite bank of the river, where several picnickers heard it and instantly started screaming in reply and running about, looking for shelter. Flocks of birds scattered from the treetops for a mile around us, and small furry animals dove underground.

"What did you DO?" I asked again.

"Nothing!" Duke said. "OK, well, I might have left the badger under a bush next to the trail…"

Waylon burst out of the trees at a run, carrying the badger by the throat. "I don't ever want to see this thing again! I almost peed on it - then I almost peed on myself when I saw it! STUPID BADGER!!" He drop-kicked the critter off the cliff and into the river.

"SPOT!!" Duke wailed. He sprinted after the badger and flung himself over the cliff.

"He named it Spot?!?" I asked.

"Good riddance!" Waylon shouted.

"You realize that cliff isn't high enough to kill him, right?"

Waylon hung his head. "I know. Dammit." He looked back at me. "But if it sinks, maybe we can get to the truck while he's diving for it. Let him get a ride back to town with the picnickers across the river."

"Would you give a ride to a total stranger who crawled out of a river carrying a dead badger?"

"Of course not. That makes leaving him behind that much better."

The badger suddenly appeared at the top of the cliff, followed by Duke's grinning face. "He floats! It looked just like he was swimming! That was awesome, dude!"

Waylon shook his head and started gathering up his things.

LATE THAT NIGHT, WAYLON TAPPED ON MY BEDROOM DOOR. "HEY," HE whispered. "You're not hungry, are you?"

"No, I'm sleeping. Why do you care if I'm hungry?"

"No reason. Just don't use the refrigerator until morning. You've been warned."

"O-kay..."

I lay in bed wondering what was going on. Half an hour passed. My curiosity had almost got the better of me when a blood-curdling scream rang out from the kitchen, followed by sounds of breaking glass and furniture being knocked over. I jumped out of bed, certain that Waylon had finally snapped and was murdering Duke.

I flipped on the light in the kitchen. Duke was sprawled in a heap under the overturned dining table. The refrigerator door hung open. The badger peered out from the bottom shelf, cracked eggs dripping goo from its nose, its wire paw pointing accusation at Duke. A broken pickle jar leaked brine across the floor. "You know," I said, flicking off the light and turning to leave, "you really shouldn't walk around the house naked like that."

2

IN THE HEARTBURN OF
THE SEA

Call him Jethro.

Some years ago - never mind how long precisely - having little or no money in his purse, and nothing particular to interest him on shore, he thought he would sail about a little and see the watery part of the world.

The only problem was, he lived hundreds of miles *from* the watery part of the world, and even if he'd had any money (or even a purse, wallet or piggy bank to hold it in), he was just a little kid, and his parents wouldn't let him go by himself. But my brother Jethro was not one to let such trivial details get in the way of his childhood dreams.

Every little kid dreams of being something cool when they grow up - usually something that is a complete departure from whatever they might be as a little kid. Jethro dreamed of sailing around the world, which was a bit of a stretch, especially since his upbringing on our suburban cow and goat farm gave him very little access to the ocean or even brief exposure to the intoxication of salt air. But Jethro is one of that rare breed who laughs in the face of reality, which means he's not easily discouraged by common sense.

Jethro's fascination with the sea began manifesting itself early in life, when he started building toy sailboats out of 2x6 boards and old plastic peanut butter jars, and then launching them in our swimming trough (our horse trough doubled as a swimming pool whenever the horses weren't drinking out of it).

Jethro would find a scrap of 2x6 about two feet long, then he'd use Dad's screwdriver to hollow out a void in the middle of it for the cabin. Then he'd cut a peanut butter tub in half from top to bottom, and jam one of the halves over the void in the board, making the cabin roof. One old piece of dowel inserted into a round hole forward of the peanut butter cabin, and he had a reasonable imitation of a model sailboat.

Jethro's scrap sailboats were virtually unsinkable, because a near-solid block of fir is about as buoyant as a beach ball. Even if you filled the little carved out cabin with water until the peanut butter jar over-flowed, the boats just wouldn't sink. Pretty good feature for a young boy's toy sailboat. Not such a good thing if that same young boy inter-prets the performance as an indication of his bright future as a marine architect.

Jethro figured that since his board-n-butter boats were unsinkable, his next logical step was to build a boat large enough to keep him afloat, too. The 2x6's weren't big enough or stable enough, and any solid log that would have been large enough would also have been too heavy for a skinny twelve year old to drag into the horse trough. Jethro needed something with volume as well as strength and buoyancy. Something watertight would have been good too, but he didn't want to get overwhelmed by details.

Jethro found a pile of plywood scraps left over from the slightly off-square extension Dad had recently added to our garage. He also found some nails, half of a can of roofing tar, and a rusty old hand saw. He went to work in a flurry of motion and a cloud of sawdust, emerging several hours later carrying his newest sailboat inverted over his head.

He staggered toward the swimming trough, the weight of the contraption threatening to snap his shins with every step. My brother Inigo, one year Jethro's senior, was waiting for him, nonchalantly leaning against the side of the trough.

"Whaddya doin'?" Inigo asked with a grin. "Cleaning out your bedroom?"

"What're you… erk… what're you talkin' about?" Jethro staggered under the weight of the sailboat. He tried to act cool, but his vertebrae were on the verge of mutiny.

"Your bedroom," Inigo said, nodding his head toward Jethro's boat. "Looks like you're planning to wash out one of your dresser drawers in the swimming trough."

"Funny," Jethro said with a gasp, dropping one corner of the boat to the ground and massaging the small of his back. "This aint no dresser drawer - it's my sailboat!"

"That don't look like a sailboat to me. Aren't sailboats supposed to have a pointy end on 'em?"

"Yeah," Jethro said, looking at the semi-rectangular craft, "but I couldn't figure out how to make the end pointy. Dad's saw is duller than a doughnut - I was lucky to get it to cut straight lines. Curves and angles woulda been impossible."

"It has straight lines?" Inigo asked. "Where?"

"Shaddap and help me launch it," Jethro said. I don't think I can lift it again by myself."

"Sure thing," Inigo said. "Just a sec." He cupped his hands around his mouth and hollered at the top of his lungs toward the house. "HEY, YOU GUYS!! JETHRO'S GONNA SAIL A DRESSER DRAWER IN THE SWIMMING TROUGH!!!!"

"Ya sap!" Jethro hissed. "Whatcha do that for?"

"Misery loves company," Inigo said as the back door slammed open and the yard quickly filled with curious siblings. "And I can't stand to see you miserable with nobody else around to enjoy it."

"I'm not miserable," Jethro said. "This'll be my finest hour. You'll see."

"Let's hope so," Inigo said. "I haven't had a good laugh in a while."

"Jethro, what are you doing with your dresser drawer out here?" My sister Sara was the oldest kid still living at home, and liked to appoint herself benevolent interim dictator anytime our parents were gone. "You're gonna get it when Daddy gets home!"

"Aint either," Jethro said. "He won't care when he sees what a cool boat I built."

"Is Jethro gonna drown?" I asked my sister Jinty, my lower lip starting to quiver. "If he drowns, we're all gonna get it!" I was never known for my optimism - not even at the tender age of four.

"Quit sniveling," Jinty said. "He's not gonna drown. He might catch an ammonia, but he's not gonna drown."

"What's an ammonia?"

"Pneumonia," my sister Galla corrected. "And he's not going to catch pneumonia from sinking a dresser drawer in the horse trough."

"Can I have your bike after you drown?" Rico asked.

"I get his bike," Inigo said. "You can have his dresser." He looked at Jethro's boat. "Well, at least you can have what's left of his dresser - one of the drawers is about to get ruined."

"IT'S NOT A DRESSER DRAWER!" Jethro shouted. "Rico, make yourself useful for once and go get me one of the oars from the Titanic II." The Titanic II was our old wooden rowboat that was currently doubling as a planter box for weeds near our pasture fence.

"Only if I get your bike," Rico said. "I don't want a dresser with one drawer missing."

"Fine!" Jethro said, exasperated. "You can have my bike after I drown!" He watched Rico run happily away. "Too bad I aint gonna drown."

"I thought I got your bike," Inigo complained. "You don't have anything else worth taking."

"You get to help me launch it," Jethro said. "You can be the First Mate."

"I'd rather be an innocent bystander, but I'll help you launch it anyway. What're you gonna use to christen it with?"

"Whaddya mean?"

"Everybody knows ya gotta christen a new boat when ya launch it," Inigo said. "You need a bottle of champagne, or something, and ya bust it over the bow as ya launch it. Which end's the bow, anyway?"

"Where am I supposed to get champagne?"

"Mom's got a 40 ouncer of Burgie beer in the fridge," Galla offered.

"That's for killing slugs," Sara said. "Not sinking scows."

"Why's Jethro gonna sink some cows?" I asked.

"Scows!" Sara and Galla chorused.

"Huh?"

"How about Pepto-Bismol?" We all turned around. My sister Lauralynn was coming out of the house with a pink bottle in her fist.

"You can't christen a ship with Pepto-Bismol!" Jethro howled.

"Might as well," Inigo said. "This thing's gonna give you heartburn when it sinks, anyway."

"Pepto's not for heartburn," Sara said. "It's for gas."

"You're all giving me heartburn AND gas!" Jethro said. "Let's just launch it, already!"

Inigo grabbed one side of the boat and helped Jethro lever it over the edge of the swimming trough. We were all a little surprised when it didn't immediately crash dive like a ballistic missile submarine on evasive maneuvers. Instead, it bobbed gently around the trough.

"Hey!" Jethro shouted. "It floats!"

We all stared at him.

"I mean, uh... See! It floats!"

"It's leaking." We all looked at my sister Emeline, who until this point had kept quiet. She was leaning over the edge of the trough, inspecting the inside of the boat. "See?" She pointed. "It's leaking like one of MP's diapers!"

"I don't wear diapers!"

"Maybe not," Sara laughed, "but the ones you used to wear leaked about like that!" The bottom of the boat was steadily filling with water. Bits of dried roofing tar floated around in the bilge, and the craft started listing to the starboard.

"Where's that clod Rico with my oar?" Jethro looked around in a panic. "Inigo, help me get it up on the side of the trough and drain it out!" Inigo shrugged and grabbed the boat by one of the gunwales - which looked more and more like the edge of a dresser drawer as the boat settled into the water. They hauled the boat out of the trough and dumped several gallons of water onto the half-dead lawn. Some of the roofing nails were working their way free from the boards, and the cheap plywood was starting to delaminate.

"Did he drown yet?" Rico came running from the cow pasture with a weatherbeaten oar in his arms.

"Gimme that oar!" Jethro yanked the oar away from Rico and tossed it in the bottom of the boat. "Alright," he said to Inigo.

"HEAVE!" They shoved the thing back over the edge of the trough, and it splashed down for the second time.

"Do ya want the Pepto now, Jethro?" Lauralynn asked.

"Cork it," Jethro said, swinging a leg over the side of the trough and into his boat. "Hold it steady, Inigo!" Inigo held the boat still, and Jethro settled gingerly into the bottom. He swung the oar over his head with a flourish, and shoved off.

The swimming trough was only about eight feet in diameter, so he didn't have far to sail - but he never made it. The roofing tar unstuck, the nails worked their way free, and the plywood dissolved into several thin sheets of flimsy laminate. Jethro went down with his ship before he made it halfway across the trough.

"Awww, man.." He groaned as the rising water finally stopped at his armpits. His left eyelid started twitching furiously.

Lauralynn whispered in Emeline's ear. "Does he want the Pepto NOW??"

"Shhhhh," Emeline whispered back. We all backed quietly away, observing an impromptu moment of silence and leaving Jethro to his grief. He sat there in his submerged drawer, muttering to himself.

ONE AFTERNOON FORTY YEARS LATER, I HAD A RARE MOMENT OF QUIET after a long commute from work. I hadn't heard from Jethro for some time, so I called him.

"Whatcha doing, dope?" I asked.

"Drinking a glass of wine, watching the sun go down," he said.

"Watching the sun go down?" I asked. "It's not even four thirty!"

"Any time after noon, the sun's officially going down. So I'm watching it."

"Shouldn't you be just getting *off* of work?"

"Only if I was a government trough-slopper like you. You forget, I'm self employed. It's quittin' time when I say it's quittin' time, and I said it was quittin' time three days ago."

"Where are you?"

"On my boat. In San Francisco. Watching the sun go down."

I gritted my teeth. In spite of the episode with the leaky dresser drawer, Jethro has always refused to listen to caution or common sense from any of his siblings. You might think that as a result he would go on to a life of disappointment and failure, but nothing could be further from the truth. Now he has *two* sailboats - he keeps the small one on a lake near his home for when he doesn't feel like driving to San Francisco. The large one he saves for making me feel foolish for pursuing a life of practicality and responsibility, since I don't have a sailboat of my own. I don't even have a spare dresser drawer to float around in.

"Why don't you ever come down and hang out on the boat with me?" Jethro was asking.

I stopped grinding my teeth for a moment. "Cuz I have a job, you clod. I can't just up and leave at the drop of a hat."

"Sucks to be you," he said. "Maybe you could just crack a bottle of wine at your house, and pretend you're hanging out on a sweet sailboat with me."

"We don't have any wine," I growled. "Besides, I hafta get up early tomorrow and go back to work."

"Bummer," he said. "How 'bout some Pepto-Bismol instead?"

"That's for gas, ya knothead. You're giving me heartburn."

"I had that once," he said. "About forty years ago."

3
SCUBA TENTING

M<small>OJO</small> <small>BURST THROUGH THE DOOR OF OUR DORM ROOM, HALF OUT OF</small> breath. "C'mon, man," he said. "Get yer junk, and let's go. Daylight's burnin'!"

"Just let me get my tent out of the wall locker," I said. "It's buried under a bunch of crap, for some reason."

"I can tell ya what the reason is," he said, exasperated. "It's on account of you tossing all yer crap in a heap when you got back from elk hunting last fall. You put stuff away, it'll be easier to find later."

"Thanks, mom."

"Just saying, man. A clean room's a happy room."

"This from the guy with a scorched pair of tighty-whities hanging on his locker door."

"Them's just evidence of an unfortunate industrial accident. I keep 'em as a reminder of how NOT to light a poot. Safety first, I always say."

"Whatever. Help me get my tent untangled from this fishing pole."

"Sloppy Airman. Forget that tent. I borrowed one from Al at work - he says it sets up in two minutes, sleeps six, and it only weighs four and a half ounces!"

"Yeah, right," I said. "You use more than four and a half ounces of toilet paper just to blow your nose. No way they can make a tent that light that'll keep any weather off of us."

"It'll be fine," Mojo said. "It aint supposed to rain for the next week. What's the worst that could happen?"

"We could die of exposure when your toilet paper tent dissolves in a heavy dew, that's what."

"Don't be such a baby. C'mon - quit wasting time! We don't get movin' now, we'll be pitching the tent at midnight."

"In that case, it's a good thing it's made outta toilet paper - maybe it'll be easier to see in the dark."

Mojo and I had decided on an overnight camping trip on the spur of the moment a day earlier, planning to camp next to a river in the mountains near the air base where we lived. It was mid-April and the weather had been beautiful all week - perfect for a spring camping trip. I finally gave up trying to free my tent and followed him downstairs to my truck. "Tell me again why I'm driving?" I asked. "I drove us fishing last week - it should be your turn."

"Maybe so, but you're the one with four-wheel drive. We'll need it, and my truck don't have it. Thusly - you're driving. It's simple math, really."

"I don't think math has anything to do with it. My truck's a pile - it barely starts anytime it rains. Something about moisture in the air makes the engine croak."

"That's 'cuz the farmer you bought it from cut all the smog equipment off it with a hacksaw. You got rooked, boy."

"Yeah, yeah. I just think we'd be better off driving your truck. At least it starts every time."

"Startin' don't do ya any good if you're stuck in a mud hole."

"I thought you said it wasn't supposed to rain - where're we gonna find a mud hole to get stuck in?"

"Damn Yankees always got an argument, my Lord…"

AN HOUR LATER WE WERE STILL ARGUING AS I CAREFULLY STEERED MY truck into the canyon where we planned to camp. The road wound down and down until ninety percent of the sky was blocked out by mountains rising on all sides. We found a wide grassy bank next to the snowmelt-flooded river - a perfect campsite. Mojo clambered out of the truck as soon as it rolled to a stop.

"That's what I'm talkin' about, boy!" he said, taking a deep breath of the cool spring air. "You set up the tent, and I'll get dinner started."

That was okay by me. Mojo was a pretty good cook, and the cheapo tent he'd borrowed looked pretty basic. I pulled it out of its stuff sack and unfolded it. "Hey, Mojo," I said. "I dunno about this tent, man. It looks *really* flimsy."

"Quit yer worryin'," he said as he set up his camp stove on the tailgate of my truck. "Gonna be a beautiful night. Have a beer and relax - I'll have us some elk steaks whipped up in no time."

"Ok, then…"

I couldn't quit worrying, though. I'd seen kites made out of sterner stuff than this tent. It looked like it wouldn't keep out an angry comment, much less any pouring rain. I glanced at the clear sky once or twice, then figured, *What's the worst that could happen?*

After I got the tent set up and Mojo finished cooking our steaks, we settled in for a relaxing evening. As we leaned against the truck, eating our dinner, we watched a huge herd of elk move across the mountainside on the opposite bank of the river. They disappeared over the ridge line, silhouetted one by one against the dying sun. We both grinned like idiots, reveling in the pristine beauty of the place.

Then the clouds started rolling in.

"Hey, man," I said. "Those clouds look pretty serious. We'd probably better button stuff up for the night."

"Yeah," Mojo said, tossing a nervous skyward glance over his shoulder. He started packing up his camp stove and lashing down loose equipment. I crawled into the tent and spread out my new sleeping bag. I had spent a good deal of money on it, and was looking forward to putting it to the test. The manufacturer claimed it was rated to 15 degrees below zero, so I was sure I'd be plenty warm.

Mojo stuck his head in the tent. "Hey man," he said. "It's startin' to snow out here!"

"SNOW?!? You said it wasn't supposed to *rain* for a week! You didn't say anything about snow!"

"That's what the weatherman claimed. How's I supposed to know he was a liar?"

"He's a weatherman. That's only one step above a used car salesman, two above a politician. They're *all* liars."

I stuck my head out of the tent and eyeballed the mountain above us. There was a clear line of white about a hundred feet above camp where the snow was already sticking on the hillside. Wet flakes swirled around camp in the wind, and the temperature was dropping noticeably.

"Forget this," I said, yanking my head back in the tent. "It's bedtime. Here's where this sleeping bag earns its keep."

Mojo crawled into the tent and looked enviously at my sleeping bag. His well-used bag had several thin spots and a couple of obvious holes in it. "You sure you don't want to trade? I'm a little tougher than you, so if that fancy bag blows out in the night, I'll be able to handle it better. It might kill the likes of you. Just sayin'."

"Thanks," I said, "but I'll take my chances. Nothing like living dangerously to build character."

"Riiight." Mojo pulled his boots off and wriggled into his sleeping bag. "Ahhhh... Ol' Betsy, don't fail me now!"

"Who's Ol' Betsy?"

"My sleeping bag, man. She's been with me through thick and thin."

"Looks more like thin and thinner," I said. "It gets much colder, you're gonna wake up frozen solid like Jack Nicholson at the end of *The Shining*. Just don't try snuggling up to me - I have a knife, and I ain't afraid to use it."

"Dream on, Yankee boy," Mojo said, laughing. "Ol' Betsy'll keep me toasty as always, and your high-dollar bag is gonna end up giving you frostbite and heartburn at the same time. How much did you pay for that thing, anyway?"

"About what I paid for my truck."

"Hope you didn't buy it offa the same farmer!" Mojo chuckled and burrowed into his moth-eaten bag. He was snoring happily a few moments later.

MY SLEEPING BAG LIVED UP TO ITS BILLING. IT WAS ACTUALLY A LITTLE *TOO* warm for comfort, so I unzipped it partway to let some of the heat out. Once I was properly ventilated, I drifted off to the sound of Mojo's buzz-saw snoring.

Somewhere in my dreams, I became aware of cold feet. That didn't make sense. This brand new bag was actually too warm - I couldn't possibly have cold feet. I shook off the idea and tried to slip back into my comfortable coma.

There it was again.

My feet felt cold.

Why did my feet feel cold?!?

I wriggled my toes around. Not only did they feel cold, but they felt kind of... wet.

Was that a splash I just heard?

What the...?

I sat up. The lower half of my sleeping bag was awash in a small river that was flowing through the front of the toilet-paper tent. I sat there a moment, stunned. Then I heard something like a small, badly tuned outboard engine, sputtering and coughing. I looked over at Mojo.

He was still asleep, laying on his side with half his face submerged in icy snowmelt. Every breath and snore caused him to blow bubbles and sputter, but he kept on sleeping. I punched him in the shoulder.

"Wake up, stupid! You're gonna drown!"

He sucked in a breath, getting half a mouth full of water at the same time. He came up coughing and shouting. "No, Momma, I SWEAR I went to the bathroom before bed!"

"You clown!" I hollered. "I'm not your mom, and you didn't wet the bed! Get up before we float out to sea!"

Mojo came to his senses. "What the... OHHH, THAT'S COOLD!! What happened?!?!?"

"You borrowed a crappy leaky tent and we pitched it in the middle of a flash flood, that's what happened! We gotta get outta here before we freeze to death!"

The floor of the tent was almost entirely awash now, and the water was rising fast. I felt like I was in third class on board the Titanic. Mojo's sleeping bag was on the downhill half of the tent, so he was worse off, but I was having a hard time getting my bag unzipped. I started flopping around frantically like a landed fish.

"Get this thing offa me!" I shouted. I rolled over and landed on top of Mojo, pinning him in his bag.

"Get off, man!" he hollered. "I don't wanna die like this! My momma'd never understand!"

"It's not my fault! This zipper's stuck and I can't get my other arm out of the bag!"

Mojo let out an animal scream, and a ripping sound emanated from deep within Ol' Betsy. He suddenly burst from his bag, shoved me to one side of the tent, and jumped to his feet. He stood there for a moment, his chest heaving and his tighty-whities drooping with damp. "SONOFA!!! It's colder than a frozen corpse in here! Where'd my boots go?"

"I think I'm laying on one of them. Get me outta this bag, dangit!" Mojo reached down and started fumbling with the frozen zipper. His fingers were shaking so violently that he couldn't get a grip on it, and several times he lost control of his hands altogether and slapped me in the face. At least, I *think* he lost control of them…

"Will you quit slapping me and get me out?!?!" I wailed after he had slapped me rapid-fire three more times.

"I'm trying! Quit thrashin' around!" He set his jaw, grabbed the zipper one last time and yanked with all he had. His hand slipped free again and he slapped me hard across the forehead. The force threw him off balance and he fell over backward, sitting down hard on top of Ol' Betsy in the middle of a huge puddle. But the zipper finally broke free.

I struggled out of the sodden bag and crawled to my feet, my teeth chattering like a machine gun. I grabbed my jeans as they floated by on the current. Mojo was dumping water out of his boot.

"You got any dry socks?" he asked, looking around for his other boot.

I looked down at my feet, ankle deep in water. "I'm wearing the dry ones. My other pair was in the bottom of my sleeping bag."

"Whadja put 'em in there for?"

"So they'd be warm when I changed into 'em in the morning, dope. I hate cold socks."

"Huh. Great idea, Einstein."

"It *was* a great idea," I said. "If I'da known we were gonna end up scuba tenting before morning, I'da put 'em someplace dry... oh, wait - THERE'S NO PLACE DRY IN THIS CRAPPY TENT!!"

"Don't blame me, man," Mojo said. "If you weren't such a sloppy Airman, you'da been able to get your fancy pants tent loose of your wall locker, and we wouldn't be in this mess."

"How is this my fault? You borrowed this thing, not me! Now pipe down and help me wring out my jeans."

"I gotta wring out my tighty-whities first. I'm turning into a dang popsicle." He skinned out of his underwear.

"Agghhh!" I wailed. "Next time, warn me before ya drop your drawers! Now I'm frozen *and* blind!"

Mojo throttled his soggy shorts, wringing a gallon and a half of icy water onto my coat as it floated past.

"Agghhh! You're sick!" I said, grabbing at my coat. "Now I'm gonna have to burn this!"

"Good," Mojo said as he stepped back into his chonies. "We could use a fire right about noweeeyyaahh-yah-ayeee!"

"Still a little cold, are they?" Now Mojo's teeth were chattering wildly. He glared at me. I hustled to wring out my clothes and get dressed, shivering the whole time like I was having a seizure. I opened the tent door and fell through it.

"What's it like out there?" Mojo asked. He was still inside, looking for his other boot.

"Sunny and warm," I said. "I'm thinking about working on my tan."

"Real funny. Just get a fire started."

"No chance," I said. The fire ring was under three inches of water.

"I'm gonna start the truck and get the heater warmed up. Get yer boots on and start slinging crap in the back so we can get outta here."

Mojo grunted agreement as I wrenched my keys out of my soggy pocket. I climbed into the truck and turned the ignition. The engine groaned and spewed a huge cloud of black smoke that enveloped Mojo and the tent - but the truck didn't start.

Mojo's head emerged from the black cloud. "Whatsa matter with that pile? You better get it started, or we're gonna die out here!"

"I told you we shoulda brought your truck!" I said. "This hunk of junk barely starts when it's not raining - if it *is* raining, it blows black smoke and runs on half a cylinder if you're lucky. START, YOU STUPID SONOFA!!!" I cranked the ignition several times. The engine coughed and sputtered, then finally caught. By now, the entire camp-ground was under a black cloud of foul smelling exhaust.

"Look at the bright side," Mojo shouted over the clattering engine. "Maybe somebody'll see all this smoke and report a forest fire. We could get a ride home on a fire truck!"

"Nobody'd believe that anything'd burn in this freakin' rain. We'd be drowned by the time they finally got to us - which might happen anyway, by the way - then we'll get a ride home in a hearse!" I feath-ered the gas pedal, trying to coax the other seven cylinders into life. Pressing the gas pedal felt like stepping on a half-deflated party balloon - there was some flabby resistance, but no corresponding response from the engine. Finally, the truck gave a deafening backfire, coughed twice and then settled into a shaky idle.

"Quick! Turn on the heater!" Mojo jumped in the passenger side and held his hands over the heater vents. "How come there's no air comin' out?"

"Hang on." I flicked the fan on. It made a noise like the death rattle of a dying walrus, then fell silent.

"REALLY?!?" Mojo was starting to get snippy.

"Let's just get our gear loaded," I said. "I don't wanta use up what little life is in the engine just sitting still." We both staggered out of the cab, back into the freezing rain. We shuffled back and forth, grabbing our gear and tossing it in a pile in the back of the truck. I collapsed the tent with all our sleeping gear still inside.

"Hey man," I said. "Help me drain this sucker!" Mojo grabbed one side of the tent and we hoisted it together, pouring gallons of water out the door. "This thing holds water better than it sheds it," I griped. "Maybe we shoulda turned it inside out before we set it up."

"I'm gonna turn Al inside out when we get back," Mojo said through chattering teeth.

Then the truck wheezed and died.

"*If* we get back," I corrected. "Keep loading - I'll try to get it started again."

TEN MINUTES LATER, THE ENGINE GROANED BACK TO LIFE. BY THAT TIME, Mojo and I were suffering from acute frostbite and smoke inhalation at the same time. We tossed the last of our gear in the back and jumped in the cab. During the drive back out to the highway, the truck never felt like it was running on more than three cylinders. On one steep incline, we barely maintained enough forward momentum to keep from rolling backward down the hill. The heater was completely dead. The windshield fogged up so badly that we had to roll down the side windows and stick our heads out to see where we were going. By the time we got to the highway, our eyebrows were covered in frost and our noses were running like rivers.

"Th-th-th-this b-b-b-blows!" Mojo said.

"N-n-n-no k-k-k-kidding," I said. "I w-w-was h-hoping we could d-d-do it again next w-w-week!"

I steered the truck up onto the highway, and we shivered all the way back to the air base. As we rolled up to the front gate in a cloud of black smoke, the guard watched us suspiciously. I rolled to a stop and held my ID badge out for him to see, but my hand was shaking so violently, the card was nothing but a blur.

"Sir, you'll have to hold it still," he said.

"That's as still as it gets," I said. Then I sneezed. The guard took a step back and put a hand on his sidearm.

"Either you hold the card still, or you'll have to get out of the vehicle," he barked.

23

"At least if he shoots you, the bullet will be warm," Mojo whispered.

"Shaddap," I said through clenched teeth. I reached my right hand over and pinned my left arm against the truck door, forcing it to be still. The guard leaned in warily and inspected the card, then compared the picture to my face.

"Sir, are you aware that you have a bright red bruise across your forehead, in the shape of a hand?"

"Yeah," I said. "I just got that today. Does it make me look taller?"

"It makes you look nothing like your ID," he said. He wasn't smiling.

"Well, that might be because my nose wasn't running as much when they took that picture," I explained, forcing a weak grin.

"Issh," the guard muttered, making a face and relaxing the grip on his pistol. "You can go through. But I think your vehicle is on fire."

"I wish," Mojo and I said in unison.

4
THE FOOT

FREYE LAKE, CASCADE MOUNTAINS
Friday, 30 Minutes Past Sundown

THE NIGHT WAS ALL-ENCOMPASSING.

I sat there in the dark, shivering slightly against the chill and nervously tending my pot of beans as it warmed on my camp stove. The light from the burner barely lit up anything farther than my feet, and the heavy silence of the forest around my camp was fast becoming ominous.

Then a twig snapped behind me.

I dropped my spoon in the pot and spun around, fumbling with my flashlight. The anemic beam barely shed light on anything farther than ten feet away. If anything, it made my paranoia worse. I could see nothing behind me but empty forest, but I knew better.

It was… The Foot.

I slowly reached for my knife.

Two Days Earlier
Wednesday, 3:00 p.m.

"Whaddaya mean, you can't go?" I asked.

Jethro looked at me with an annoying smirk. "Just what I said, sap. Get the wax outta yer ears, and I won't hafta repeat myself."

"Clod, you said last week that you weren't doing anything this weekend. You've never been to Freye Lake, and you *know* you want to climb McLoughlin again. What's your problem?"

"That was last week," Jethro said, "before I made other plans. We got a free weekend in a timeshare in Reno."

"Issh," I made a face. "Reno's lousy with picnickers. Whaddaya want to go there for?"

"Free buffet. Why else?"

"Sissy."

"Nice try," Jethro sneered, "but even you can't shame me out of free food. Find somebody else to go with you."

Problem was, I'd already invited everybody else I knew, and they had all taken the sissy way out - from making up lame excuses to just not returning my calls.

"Fine," I said. "Enjoy bellying up to the buffet line. Maybe you won't die of salmonella. I'll go to Freye Lake by myself."

"By yourself?" Jethro was skeptical. "You can't even find your way to the mailbox by yourself. You're gonna get lost and die of exposure."

"It's August, moron. One night in a tent isn't going to over-expose me."

"Ok, then. You're gonna get eaten by The Foot instead."

"Your threats don't scare me. The Foot's a vegetarian."

"Not when he's really hungry. Then he thinks people taste like chicken."

"That makes no sense. Chickens are made outta meat too, in case you hadn't noticed."

"So?"

"So - if The Foot's a vegetarian, how would he know what chicken tastes like?"

"He's a selective vegetarian. He likes his veggies with a side of meat."

"You're a moron."

"Says you. Can I have your truck after you die of exposure and get eaten by The Foot?"

THURSDAY, 5:30 P.M.

"YOU'RE GOING ALONE?"

"Yeah, Mom," I said, rolling my eyes at the phone.

"You're gonna die of exposure."

"Thanks for the vote of confidence," I said. "Jethro thinks I have an even chance of surviving exposure, but then I'll get eaten by The Foot."

"Jethro's not very bright," she said. *"The Foot's a vegetarian."*

"That's what I told him - he wouldn't listen."

"But being a vegetarian doesn't mean he'll let you live. Probably throttle you in your sleep for trespassing in his forest."

"You're a regular little ray of sunshine, you know that?"

"That's what they say. Can I have your lawnmower after The Foot throttles you to death?"

I hung up the phone.

FRIDAY, 1:45 P.M.

"BIG PLANS THIS WEEKEND?" MY BOSS SMILED AT ME, WAITING expectantly. He was always just a little too interested in what I did outside of work. He was also overly cautious and unnaturally timid - a classic picnicker.

"Gonna climb Mt. McLoughlin," I said, pulling a stack of plastic water pipes off a truck and turning to take them into the warehouse.

"Isn't that dangerous?" He was not the adventurous type, to say the least.

"Only if you're a picnicker," I muttered.

"What's that?"

"I said, 'only if you're not careful.' McLoughlin's a walk-up. Don't need ropes or anything."

"Oh. So, you're leaving in the morning?"

"Nope," I said, hefting another stack of pipe. "Right after work today."

"But, you don't get off 'til two," he said, confused. "How will you have time to drive out there, climb the mountain, and get back before dark?"

I dropped the pipes onto the growing stack. "I won't. I'm not climbing the mountain until tomorrow morning. Tonight I'll drive out and hike into a little lake part way up the trail. I'll camp out there, and get an early start tomorrow."

"Who are you going with?"

"Nobody. I couldn't find any non-sissies, so I'm going by myself."

He looked horrified. "By yourself?!? That can't be safe!"

"Who said anything about safe? It'll be fun!" I was starting to enjoy his discomfort.

"But what if something happens?"

"What could happen?"

"Your truck could break down!"

"So I'll walk."

"You could break a leg!"

"Then I'll crawl."

"What if you get abducted?"

"Who'd want me?"

"You never know." He threw a suspicious glance around the loading dock. "There's sickos out there, you know."

"There's sickos around here, too," I said under my breath.

"What's that?"

"I said, 'it's near two.' Almost quitting time."

"What if you run into a Sasquatch?"

"I'll get his autograph for ya."

"I heard they're dangerous. Maybe *they'd* want to abduct you."

"I'd have a better chance of getting abducted by aliens than by The Foot."

"The what?"

"The Foot. You know - Sasquatch, Bigfoot - The Foot."

"Well, what if one decides to eat you?"

"They don't eat people - they're vegetarians."

"How do you know that?"

"Everybody knows that. You know anybody that's ever been eaten by a Foot?"

"Well, no…"

"There ya go. Vegetarians."

"I dunno, still sounds dangerous to be out there all by yourself. Get one of the other guys to go with you, at least."

"What are you, my mother? No wait, my mother doesn't even worry about me this much. You need a hobby. It'll help take your mind offa my private life."

"I'm just concerned about my employee, that's all. So, can I have your coffee cup after you get abducted and eaten by The Sasquatch?"

Sigh.

"The Foot," I corrected him. "They prefer to be called The Foot. And stay away from my coffee cup."

By this time, I was getting really annoyed. Not only was nobody willing to come with me on my hike, but to a person, everybody I talked to about it was trying to discourage *me* from going.

Sissies.

Picnickers.

Didn't they know the joy of adventure? The wonder of discovery? Too many people were focusing on non-existent dangers, and forgetting the thrill of doing something unique, something exciting and slightly risky that most people would go out of their way to avoid.

I smiled to myself as I hid my coffee cup behind a box of pipe fittings and clocked out. My boss shook his head sadly at me as I walked past him to my truck.

"If you're not back on Monday morning, I'll have to hire a replacement," he called out.

"Maybe I'll stay in the woods for good," I said over my shoulder. "If I do, I'll send a Foot back here to take my place. You're always saying I can be replaced with a small furry animal."

"But The Sasquatch is a *large* furry animal!"

"So much the better. You get more furry animal, and I get to retire early. See you on Monday. Maybe."

MT. MCLOUGHLIN TRAILHEAD
Friday, 4:30 p.m.

I SHOULDERED MY PACK AND TURNED TO START UP THE TRAIL. IT WAS A beautiful afternoon - warm but not hot. The air had a sweet smell, and the birds were singing happily.

Then I tripped over a root and fell flat on the trail as my top-heavy pack slid up on my shoulders and drove my face into the dirt.

"Sonofa..." I rolled over and struggled to my feet. As I re-adjusted my gear, I thought I heard soft laughter. I spun around, looking into the trees on either side.

Nothing.

I had to be hearing things. There were no other vehicles at the trailhead, and the only other access to the trail was miles away. Nobody else could be out here this late in the day. I took a last look around, and set off again.

TWENTY MINUTES LATER, I ROUNDED A BEND IN THE TRAIL AND surprised a large deer. He took three quick jumps to get out of my reach, then stopped and looked at me over his shoulder. I watched him for a moment, thrilled to be so close to some wildlife.

Then the deer bared his teeth at me and sneezed.

Oddly though, it looked almost like he had smiled and laughed.

I watched him trot away. He seemed to be in no hurry, and kept looking back at me, grinning and sneezing in my general direction.

Stupid deer.

I continued on, trying to forget about it. Deer don't laugh. I was imagining things.

When I finally reached Freye Lake, I'd forgotten the smart aleck deer. I had the entire lake to myself, and the lone campsite on the east shore gave me a tantalizing view of the summit of Mt. McLoughlin. It was a perfect setting. After I set up camp, I sat down next to a log, stretched out my legs and watched the sunset. The peak of Mt. McLoughlin was in silhouette as the shadows around me grew, and the late afternoon sky was tinted a pale blue.

Beautiful.

FRIDAY, HALF AN HOUR PAST SUNSET

I WOKE WITH A START TO THE SOUND OF SOFT LAUGHTER.

I sat up and looked around. The light was almost completely gone. I had slept for a couple of hours, at least - now I was running out of daylight and I still hadn't had dinner! I scrambled to my feet and hustled around, trying to get my stove going before it got too dark to see. I couldn't have a campfire - the southern Oregon woods in August are typically dryer than a biscotti in a blast furnace - so the only source of light I had was a puny little flashlight and the burner on my camp stove. I frantically worked the pump on the stove, trying to get enough pressure to make the fuel flow to the burner.

Suddenly there was a loud *thump* right behind me.

I yelped and spun around, kicking the stove over in the process. The burner pan filled with dirt and rocks, and half my fuel leaked out on the ground. There was nothing behind me, except for a chipmunk doing his level best to look nonchalant. I threw a pine cone at him. It sailed high and outside, and the chipmunk yawned.

Stupid rat.

I set the stove upright and got it lit. The chipmunk moved over onto a fallen log and watched me, occasionally washing his face with his tiny paws as I worked. I kept hearing noises in the woods around me, but in the failing light it was impossible to pinpoint the source. I turned back to my stove, putting a pot of beans on to warm.

THUMP.

I spun around again, only to find the chipmunk ignoring me and inspecting his fingernails. "Beat it, vermin," I said. I slung another pine cone at him and he scampered behind my tent.

My beans were starting to steam. I took a pull from my water bottle as I stirred them, struggling against the urge to keep looking over my shoulder.

Something splashed in the lake. Something *large*.

I looked out at the water, straining my eyes to make out details in the gloom. It was almost pitch black now, impossible to see anything other than the distinct absence of light surrounding my camp.

Then a twig snapped behind me.

I dropped my spoon into the pot and grabbed my flashlight. I snapped it on, and it chose that moment to develop a short circuit. The beam flickered and died as I tried to scan the woods. I pounded the flashlight against my free hand, hoping to beat it back to life. It came back on just long enough to reveal something large and hairy standing behind a tree not ten feet away - then the light went out.

I froze. By this time, irrational terror had abducted my reason and was slowly throttling it to death as I sat by, helpless to do anything about it. I madly flicked the flashlight switch back and forth with one hand, trying to revive it while I slowly groped around for my knife with the other hand. I couldn't help wondering what good it would do if the light *did* come back on - did I really want to see the Foot right before he took a big bite out of me? Wouldn't it be better to not see it coming? I couldn't help it - I flicked the switch back and forth so fast, it sounded like a cop Tasering a terrorist - but the light still didn't come on.

By now, my beans were burning, but I ignored them. The imminent threat of being forcibly adopted by a family of practical-joking Feet trumped even the worst hunger cramps. *STUPID FLASHLIGHT! WORK, CURSE YOU!!*

I was looking at the flashlight in my hand, trying to diagnose the malfunction in spite of my blindness, when it suddenly came on and shone out into the forest. I slowly raised my eyes.

The beam was directed at the tree where the large hairy creature had been lurking a few moments before, but the only thing there was a ragged hank of Old Man's Beard - wispy moss that grows on trees all over the Pacific Northwest. Not possible. I *knew* I had seen something standing there. I rubbed my eyes with the back of my hand and looked again.

Nothing.

Then I heard laughter again.

Saturday, Half an Hour Before Sunrise

As the eastern sky slowly went from black to gray, the watery light revealed a hollow shell of a man cowering on the ground next to a log, shivering with the cold and flinching at every little noise. His countenance was a contorted mass of facial tics, some frozen in place, others still rapidly quivering. An untouched pot of burned beans sat on a cold camp stove that had long before run out of fuel. The trembling man occasionally flicked the switch on a burnt-out flashlight clenched in his left hand. In his right hand he wielded a spoon, erratically thrusting it like a knife at nothing in particular in front of him. Behind him on the log, a chipmunk sat nibbling a pine cone. A large deer walked slowly through the camp, pausing to stare at the man for a few moments before turning and walking into the forest. Before it vanished, it looked back over its shoulder, bared its teeth, and sneezed. Soft laughter drifted out from the cover of the trees.

The man didn't notice.

5
MEAT SANDWICHES

JETHRO POURED HIMSELF A CUP OF COFFEE AS I STOOD IMPATIENTLY WAITING at his front door. "Ya dope," I chided. "We don't have time for you to have another cup of coffee. We're gonna be late! Pour that swill in a travel mug and let's get outta here!"

Jethro hefted the ceramic cup and blew on his coffee. "This *is* my travel mug," he said. "Lids are for sissies."

"We'll see if you still think so when you spill that sludge in your lap before you get out of the driveway."

Jethro snorted. "Just 'cuz you're uncoordinated doesn't mean the rest of us are, too. Real men drive and drink coffee at the same time. *I* drive, drink coffee *and* dunk doughnuts in my coffee at the same time. Ya can't dunk a doughnut if yer travel mug has a lid on it."

"Your wife's gonna punch you in the forehead when she finds out you're taking her coffee cups duck hunting."

"I take her coffee cups everywhere. She doesn't mind. At least not until she runs out of coffee cups. I just hafta remember to bring 'em back before we have company. It's bad form to serve coffee to your guests in a cereal bowl."

"Tell me about it," I said, tipping back the cereal bowl and draining the last of my coffee. "Especially if you don't bother washing the cereal bowl first."

"That bowl was clean," Jethro protested. "Chumley licked it out last night."

"GAAgghh!" Chumley was Jethro's buffalo-esque Newfoundland dog. He was notorious for licking things that didn't belong to him. I put the bowl on the counter and tried to block out the idea of drinking coffee out of the dog dish. A subject change was in order. "Did you pack yer lunch yet, clod?"

"Sure I did. I made a meat sandwich that'd choke a horse."

"Horses don't eat meat, moron."

"That's why they'd choke on my sandwich." He looked around the kitchen. "Where *is* my sandwich, anyway?" The counter held nothing but my empty cereal/coffee bowl and a few loose crumbs. "I put it right there!"

We stared at the crumbs for a moment. Then I looked at Chumley, who was sprawled in the middle of the floor, feigning sleep. He cracked an eye open and belched at me. I grinned. "Good boy, Chumley!"

"BAD BOY, CHUMLEY!" Jethro snarled. "That sandwich had about three pounds of meat in it! Stupid dog!"

"You left a meat sandwich in his reach, and he ate it," I said. "So tell me who's the stupid one again?"

"You are. Now shaddap and help me make another sandwich."

———

HAVING A MEAT SANDWICH HANDY IS KEY FOR ANY SUCCESSFUL OUTDOOR adventure. Duck hunting, hiking, camping or just getting lost in the woods takes a lot of energy, and the best way to energize yourself is by wolfing down huge sandwiches packed with some kind of meat. No watercress, cucumber, or any other type of frilly, low-calorie, metro-sexualized sissy filling will do - real men eat meat sandwiches.

Unfortunately, there has been a disturbing trend against the use of meat sandwiches by the outdoor food industry in recent years. Mass produced camp food has gone from being mostly meat-based to being mostly sissy-based.

Tofu-laden granola bars proliferate in outdoor sections of grocery stores, and the ones not loaded with tofu are mostly inedible bricks of sawdust held together with honey-flavored glue. Meat based snacks are looked down on and openly discouraged by swarms of picnickers masquerading as outdoorsmen, and the options for real outdoor food get more limited by the day.

I even saw an advertisement recently for soy jerky. *SOY JERKY??!??* Is this what western civilization has come to? Meatless meat?? Even a dog like Chumley would turn up his immense nose at meatless meat. Dogs are dumb, but they're not stupid. They'll eat garbage if they have to, but they prefer real food.

Meat sandwiches are real food.

MEAT SANDWICHES ONCE PLAYED A CRITICAL ROLE WHEN JETHRO AND OUR brother Rico attempted an overnight hike of Mt. Shasta in northern California. True to habit, Jethro had refused to take the trail, instead leading Rico over glaciers, crevasses and raging rivers on an unmarked path chosen to avoid the herds of picnickers crowding the Forest Service yak route. By the time they reached their campsite in the middle of an impassible field of gigantic boulders, Rico was fed up.

"Idiot!" he said, throwing himself down on a boulder. "We're gonna die up here! Why can't we take the trail, like everybody else?"

"'Cuz everybody else is a picnicker," Jethro said. "What are you whining about, anyway? You said this was a good idea!"

"That was before we left town. Everything's a good idea before you actually try it. *Your* ideas always turn bad right after they start."

"Crybaby. You'll feel better in the morning. Lucky for you we're camping right here."

"HERE??" Rico looked around. "The ground here is almost straight up! What are we supposed to do, lash ourselves to a boulder so we don't roll away in our sleep?"

Jethro grinned. "Some mountaineer you turned out to be. Hope you're not planning on whining all night - you might disturb my beauty sleep."

Rico pulled a bag of greasy pepperoni chunks out of his pack and offered it to Jethro, who took a piece and eyed it suspiciously. "You could sleep longer than Rapunzel, and it wouldn't help your beauty any," Rico said. "You're not exactly easy on the eyes, ya know."

"Rumpelstiltskin," Jethro said.

"Rumple-whose skin?"

"Stiltskin. Rumpelstiltskin. He's the guy that overslept by about a hundred years. You're mixing up your fairy tales. Rapunzel was the babe in the tower with the hundred foot hair."

"Whatever. You've got several thousand foot-hairs, so Rapunzel fits you better. Except you're not a babe."

Jethro took a bite of the pepperoni. "GAAACCKKK! Where'd you get this stuff? It's vile!"

"What's the matter with it?"

Jethro paused in mid-gag. "It tastes like the butcher scraped it off the floor of the rendering plant, that's what."

"So what did you bring?" Rico asked. "Mac and cheese? Good luck cooking in this hurricane."

"'Course I didn't bring mac and cheese. I brought meat sandwiches."

"What kind?"

"Who cares? They're meat wrapped in bread. What else could you want?"

"I could want this nasty pepperoni to blow off the mountain so I don't hafta smell it any more." Rico put the pepperoni bag on a rock. "Gimme one of those sandwiches."

"Didn't you bring any other food?"

"Sure I did," Rico said. "I was just planning on eating your food first. That way, when you fall in a crevasse, I'll still have enough chow to get me home safe."

Jethro handed him a sandwich. "If I fall in a crevasse, I'm gonna make sure you fall in with me. That way I'll have something soft to land on."

"What's this?" Rico asked, peering dubiously at the sandwich bag.

"Tuna fish on blueberry bagel," Jethro said.

"That's sick!" Rico wailed. "That's not how ya make a meat sandwich! Don't you have any taste buds?"

"Taste buds are for sissies."

Jethro is a firm believer in meat sandwiches, but his sandwiches are often, shall we say, unconventional.

Rico handed the bag back to Jethro. "Thanks for nothing. Now I'm gonna hafta break into my secret stash." He turned away and rummaged in his pack.

"What's that?" Jethro asked, trying to see over Rico's shoulder. "Is that… PUDDING?!?"

"So what?" Rico said, defensive. "Pudding-packs are the best for hiking. All ya need is a spoon!"

"You rip me for making meat sandwiches outta fish, and you brought PUDDING? I *knew* you were a picnicker!"

"Picnickers pack pâté, not pudding, ya putz."

Jethro took a bite of his sandwich. "I'd rather eat pâté than that fake pudding."

"Hey, look at that!" Rico pointed uphill behind Jethro.

Jethro spun around. "What?"

"There was a beaver on that rock behind you."

"A what?"

"It was a mountain beaver. Looked like he was puttin' the sneak on ya."

"There aren't any beavers up here. What would they eat?"

"I dunno. Maybe they like tuna. There he is again!"

Jethro looked again. "That's not a beaver, ya idgit! It's a whistle-pig!"

"Is that like a Rumple-whose-skin?"

"No, fool. It's a whistle-pig. You know, a rock chuck. Marmot? Groundhog? Don't you know anything?"

"I know that thing looks a lot like a beaver. A *hungry* beaver. Quick - throw one of your fishberry sandwiches at him."

"I'm not wasting a perfectly good meat sandwich on a whistle-pig. Why don't you feed him your pudding, tough guy?"

"Two reasons," Rico said. "One, I like my pudding, and two, mountain beavers don't have opposable thumbs."

"What does that have to do with anything?"

"How's he supposed to hold the spoon without opposable thumbs?"

"Look, he left," Jethro said, pointing. "Must've heard you talking about feeding him toxic pudding."

"More like he got a whiff of that vile pepperoni."

"We should leave it on a rock downwind of camp," Jethro said. "The smell is gonna make me hurl. Maybe he'll come back for it."

"If he does, he'll have to come back for the antacid, too. I know I sure could use some."

"I'm going to sleep," Jethro said, stashing his third tuna-berry sandwich in his pack. "We need to get an early start in the morning."

"What if that mountain beaver comes back?" Rico asked. "He'll probably chew through the jerky bag, then chew through our jugular veins as payback for giving him indigestion."

"Mountain beavers aren't carnivorous," Jethro said, rolling out his sleeping bag. "But Sasquatches are."

"If I wake up to that pig-chuck gnawing on my ears, I'm gonna twist his little head off. He'll think *I'm* a Sasquatch."

"I already think you're a Sasquatch," Jethro said. "You smell like one, and that pepperoni sure tasted like Sasquatch chow."

HOURS LATER, JETHRO WOKE TO RATTLING SOUNDS ON THE WIND. HE SAT up and looked over at Rico's pack. A plastic grocery bag was retreating up the mountain.

"Rico, wake up!" He punched Rico in the kidney.

"OW!" Rico sat up. "Ya dope! What's the matter with you?"

"Your mountain beaver came back and made off with your pepperoni." He pointed uphill at the now-empty grocery sack. "See?"

"Good," Rico said, laying back down. "I hope it hardens his arteries. Maybe now we can get some sleep."

"It's almost dawn anyway, sap. We might as well get up and have breakfast."

"Are you kidding?" Rico whined. "I didn't sleep a wink." He rolled over. "What's for breakfast, anyway?"

"What else?" Jethro asked, opening his pack. "Meat sandwiches!"

Rico groaned. "I already told ya, you can't make a proper meat sandwich with fruit and fish. That's just disgusting."

"So what are you gonna eat for breakfast?"

"Canned peaches."

"You hauled a bunch of canned peaches up here? What are you, some kind of masochist?"

"I must be," Rico said. "I keep going backpacking with you."

"Hey!" Jethro shouted, sticking his face deep into his pack. "My meat sandwich is missing!"

"Looks like the mountain beaver had friends over," Rico said. "He musta been desperate, to take that nasty thing."

"Shaddap and gimme some of your peaches," Jethro said.

"I'm all out," Rico said. "But I brought an extra pudding-pack."

"How can you be all out of peaches already? You haven't even rolled out of bed yet!"

"I ate breakfast three hours ago. I told you I couldn't sleep."

Jethro gnashed his teeth. "Idgit! Gimme that pudding-pack!"

Rico got out of bed and tossed a pudding cup at Jethro. Then the whistle-pig popped up from behind a rock, watching them.

Jethro glared at it. "You're not gettin' my pudding, ya little beggar!" He peeled the top off the pudding, then stopped short. "Hey! How am I supposed to eat this stuff? Got an extra spoon, clod?"

Rico was making a dramatic show of licking his plastic spoon. "Nope. Use your finger."

"I don't wanna stick my finger in my pudding!"

"Why not? You stick it in yer nose all the time - that doesn't seem to bother you."

"You're not half as funny as you think you are," Jethro said, scooping a dollop of pudding out with his finger. The whistle-pig held up a crust of bagel and munched it happily. Jethro hurled a rock at it. "Stupid mountain beaver! That's MY meat sandwich!"

"I'd rather eat a meat sandwich made outta mountain beaver than one made outta tuna berries," Rico said. "That rat probably saved your life."

"Saved my life? He ate all my food! How are we supposed to get to the summit today without any meat sandwiches? We're gonna starve up here!"

"That's why I'm not planning to *stay* up here," Rico said as he licked his pudding spoon clean for the last time. "I'm going home."

Jethro struggled to bite back his frustration. "We can't go back! We have to get to the summit, ya sissy!"

Rico stuffed his sleeping bag in his pack. "That's probably what Robert Scott told his men when they ran out of food halfway to the South Pole. Then they all ended up with terminal freezer burn, 'cuz they didn't know when to quit. *I* know when to quit, and it's right now."

"You can't quit now!" Jethro wailed.

"Sure I can," Rico said. "Hide and watch." He looked back at Jethro. "Look, stoop. If you come with me now, we'll stop at a drive-through on the way home and get half a dozen cheeseburgers. That way, you still get to eat some meat sandwiches, and I don't get to die of exposure."

Jethro pouted. "Fine. But we're coming back next weekend. I'm not gonna let some kleptomaniac mountain beaver run *me* off."

SOME HOURS LATER, THE TRAUMA OF THE CLIMB WAS FADING FAST WITH THE help of meat sandwiches. Jethro munched happily on a gut-bomb burger and started reminiscing. "That was a great climb! We went where no picnicker has gone before! That sissy MP is gonna be sad he stayed home."

"Maybe he'll come along next time," Rico said. "Once he sees how much fun we had, he won't be able to wimp out."

"Oh, he'll find a way. We'll just hafta bribe him with meat sandwiches!" He waved his burger in the air like a cudgel.

Rico flicked a pickle off of his shirt. "Watch where you're waving that thing! I have a better idea - let's make MP bring the sandwiches, and then get him to think it was his idea."

"Why do you want him to bring the sandwiches?"

"'Cuz if you bring 'em, they'll be made outta peanut butter and roadkill. If MP brings 'em, he'll put real meat inside, and I still won't have to do any work. I don't trust you around any kind of cooking."

"Good idea," Jethro said around a mouthful of burger. "But you're still a sissy for not trying tuna on blueberry bagel."

"I'm trying not to throw up just thinking about it," Rico said with a grimace. "Good thing we found these grease burgers to distract me."

Rico knew the truth - real adventures call for real food.

Real adventurers - eat meat sandwiches.

6

HOT STUFF

"WHAT A PACK OF SISSIES," I SAID, LOOKING AROUND AT MY COWORKERS. Several of them were gathered around a jar of habanero peppers that somebody had brought back from a vacation.

"You *can't* eat those," someone said with near reverence. "They're way too hot!"

The owner of the jar removed the lid and took a tentative whiff of the contents. His eyes immediately welled up and he thrust the jar away from his face. "Gaaaahhh! That's unbelievable! I betcha none of you guys can even handle a taste of the brine!"

"You first," another brave soul offered.

"You guys are really pathetic," I said, as the owner dipped a finger in the liquid. He brought it timidly to his mouth and extended his tongue a fraction of an inch. He looked like a kid taunting an angry chimpanzee at the zoo, afraid he'd get his tongue yanked out if he showed too much of it. He touched his finger to his tongue and immediately started coughing and choking. His face went red and beads of sweat ran down his forehead as he doubled over, gagging. The rest of the crew laughed and hooted with glee. It was more than I could stand.

I pushed through the onlookers, grabbed the jar and plucked a whole pepper from inside. The others quickly forgot the jar owner, who by that time was convulsing and sneezing like he'd been tear gassed. Now they were focused on me as I held the pepper up in front of my nose. I paused just long enough for dramatic effect, then opened my mouth, stuck the entire pepper inside and bit it off at the stem.

A collective gasp went up.

I casually flicked the stem into the trash can as I munched on my pepper. "Crybabies," I said. "It's not even that hot."

They all stared at me slack jawed.

"How'd you do that?" one asked.

"Doesn't it burn?" said another.

"Nah," I said with a grin. "Good flavor. It's a little warm, but not too bad."

On the outside I was the picture of cool composure, but on the inside, my digestive tract was screaming bloody murder at my brain. *YOU FOOL! WHAT HAVE YOU DONE?!???!?*

I'd never had a habanero until that moment.

I've always liked spicy food, so the spectacle of several grown men going into convulsions at the mere sight of a jar of harmless looking peppers had been more than I could take. It seemed like the perfect opportunity to shame them and make myself look cool, but at that moment it was all I could do not to curl up in the fetal position and suck my thumb in self pity. That little habanero made the hottest jalapeño taste like tofu - my mouth and throat were on fire, and the rest of my insides were already cringing, knowing they were next.

The things we do to impress people.

MY LOVE OF ALL THINGS SPICY BEGAN WHEN I WAS A KID, AND OUR MOST common summer lunch menu item was bean with bacon soup. It wasn't common because it was delicious - I always thought canned dog food would probably taste about the same or better than bean with bacon soup - it was common because there were a lot of kids in our family, and my mother bought soup by the case at the local grocery wholesaler for about three and a half cents a can. Even at that price, she was still getting ripped off.

Bean with bacon soup is nasty.

The only way to make the vile stuff palatable was to add spices - lots of them. Early on, I discovered that copious amounts of black pepper and Tabasco Sauce could mask the horrible flavor almost to the point of tolerability, so I took to doctoring my soup every time. I ended up using enough spice to make road kill taste like rack of lamb, and in the process developed a love for pepper and hot sauce. Nowadays, I'll always choose the spicy version of any food over any other option - the hotter the better.

My friend Lloyd shared my love of spicy food, and put his predilection to the ultimate test once in an Indian restaurant in Egypt. The Air Force had sent us to Egypt for several months, and we took every opportunity while we were there to sample the local food.

Egyptian food is fantastic - very flavorful with a strong Mediterranean influence - but it's not particularly spicy. So when we found an Indian restaurant at a hotel in Cairo, we were eager for some real heat. Standing outside the door, the aromas of multiple varieties of curry, peppers and exotic unknown spices wafted over us. Lloyd had a beatific grin on his face as he walked in, and my stomach started an excited growling.

The maître d' showed us to a table, saying how happy he was to have us in his restaurant. By this time my stomach was threatening to gnaw its way out of my abdomen and go off in search of food on its own. We looked at the menu for a few moments before a waiter came over.

"Yes, my friends, welcome! How may I help you?"

Lloyd studied his menu for a moment, apparently deep in thought. "What do you have that's spicy?"

The waiter smiled. "Oh yes, my friend, all our food is very spicy! The best! You will see. What would you like?"

Lloyd shook his head slowly. "No, see - I don't want just *regular* spicy. I want something *really* spicy."

The waiter's smile fell a fraction of an inch, as if to say *Oh great, this guy is gonna be one of those people you just can't satisfy* - but he recovered quickly. "Yes yes my friend, you will be very pleased with our food - very spicy, for sure!"

45

Lloyd put his menu down and shook his head. "I'd like to speak to the chef, please."

The waiter's face fell in horror, like Lloyd was a bum off the street who'd just walked into a mafia boss's living room and demanded to see Vinny the Knee Breaker. "Yes yes," he mumbled. "Of course, my friend." He backed away and disappeared into the kitchen.

"What are you doing?" I asked.

"Ordering dinner," Lloyd said. "What does it look like I'm doing?"

"Looks like you're ruining that waiter's day to me. If I hear a gunshot from the back alley, I'm outta here. Why can't you just order off the menu like every other normal person?"

"Cuz every other normal person only gets to eat the boring menu food, that's why. I'm gonna get something special."

"You're probably gonna get dragged off and interrogated for two days, naked under a bare light bulb in the chef's cellar. Then they'll toss you in the Nile so the crocodiles can have something special."

"You're sort of a pessimist, you know that?"

I opened my mouth to deny it, but the kitchen door flew open and derailed my train of thought. A large man with a face like a storm cloud burst out. He was wearing all white, with a starched chef's hat perched high on his head. His single bushy eyebrow was screwed down so far it almost looked like a second floor addition to his mustache. Our waiter was close on his heels, pleading excitedly in Arabic. The chef ignored him and drew himself up in front of our table.

"Is there a problem, my friends?" His voice was polite but his look was pure murder.

"Not at all, my friend," Lloyd said with a smile. "We were just telling our waiter what a wonderful place this is, and how excited we were to have some really spicy food."

"Layin' it on a little thick, don't you think?" I whispered.

"Quiet, you," Lloyd hissed. He looked back at the chef. "I was just wondering what the spiciest dish on your menu might be?"

The chef glared at the waiter, as if to say *must I do your job as well as mine?* Then he looked back at Lloyd with a pinched smile. "My friend, any of our dishes will be spicy enough to satisfy you, I am sure.

Please, simply choose one, and I will be happy to prepare it for you myself."

Lloyd smiled. "I like my food *very* spicy."

"Yes of course, my friend," the chef said. "As I said, all of our dishes…"

"You don't understand," Lloyd interrupted, his best benevolent smile wide on his face. "I want to *cry*."

The chef looked at Lloyd, then at me, then at the waiter. Then he broke out in a smile of his own, but it was something less than benevolent. "Oh, my friend," he said. "*You will cry*." He did a quick about-face and disappeared into the kitchen.

"Nice work," I said. "Now he's gonna call sixteen of his angriest cousins, then poison our food while he waits for 'em to get here."

"Don't be such a crybaby," Lloyd said. "You can't have any fun if you go all the way to another country and then just order off the menu. You gotta take risks, try something new."

"Oh, I agree. Getting thrown into a crocodile-infested river by an enraged mob will definitely be new for me. You should be a travel guide."

"You'll thank me later, trust me."

"I won't thank you later, and I don't trust you now." I stood up. "I'm leaving before the fun starts… ooohh, bread!" The waiter had returned and plunked a huge platter of *naan*, a delicious oven-baked flatbread, on the table. I sat back down.

"What about the chef's killer cousins?" Lloyd asked.

"They can get their own bread," I said around a mouthful of naan.

"What about the crocodiles?"

"I bet they taste good on naan. With hot sauce. And lots of peppers." My outlook had changed drastically with the arrival of food.

Lloyd stuffed a second piece of naan in his mouth. "This stuff is amazing," he said. "The chef can go ahead and poison us for all I care, as long as he brings more naan first."

Just then the waiter and the chef emerged from the kitchen, shrouded in a billowing cloud of steam and wheeling a cart ahead of them. Every head in the restaurant turned in our direction. Conversation stopped dead. The chef had a wicked grin on his face.

47

"My friends, you ask me to make you cry, so I must make you cry. Anything for my friends. So for you especially, I have prepared my exclusive lamb curry!"

He whipped the lid off of a large serving bowl, revealing a steaming, bubbling mass of meat. It was covered in a brownish-red sauce, the color you might get if you roasted a red pepper just short of the point of combustion. The waiter took two wary steps back, and the chef held the lid in front of him like a shield. Waves of oily steam boiled over our table. Lloyd and I both instantly started pouring sweat. I looked at Lloyd and noticed that his nose was running steadily. Sweat dripped from his right earlobe, and he was struggling to loosen a button on his shirt. I had the strange sensation that I was the lamb, and somebody had left me in the oven with the curry a bit overlong.

It was amazing.

I blinked fast, trying to clear my eyes of the tears that wouldn't stop welling up.

"You first," Lloyd said.

"No way," I said. "This was your bright idea. Dig in, Captain Risky."

"My friends," the chef said, feigning disappointment while trying to hide a smirk behind the serving lid. "Please, do not offend my kitchen staff - they have all worked very hard to please you with this special dish!"

I looked through the fumes toward the kitchen door. Several blurry faces peered back at me. They looked like they were grinning, but I couldn't be sure.

"Have *they* tried eating this?" I asked.

"Oh, no my friend," the chef said. "This is a special privilege we reserve only for our *most favored* guests. We would not waste such an opportunity, er, delicacy on such as ourselves. Please - we will be very hurt if you do not try it."

"I think we're gonna be very hurt if we *do* try it," I muttered.

Lloyd took a deep breath. "I'm in." He took another piece of naan in one hand and ladled some of the curry onto his plate with the other. "Oh, wow," he said, wiping his brow. "I can't see! You're gonna have to feed me, MP."

"Only thing I'm feeding you is a boot to the head for getting me into this." I ladled a mound of curry onto my own plate, recoiling as my vision went all white. Oddly, the smell was powerfully enticing in spite of the temporary blindness brought on by the vapor. My stomach growled louder, ignoring the mixed messages the rest of my senses were shouting at it.

My body knows no caution where hunger is concerned.

I blinked furiously, clearing my vision just enough to make out my plate. I dipped a piece of naan into the curry, scooping up a chunk of lamb and about a teaspoon of sauce. Lloyd did the same. We looked at each other for a nervous moment - then we took a bite.

My life flashed before my eyes. I couldn't close my mouth to chew, nor could I command my tongue to spit it out. But for some reason, I didn't *want* to spit it out. It was delicious and tortuous at the same time. Random staccato pictures flashed across my mind's eye. Flame throwers, nuclear explosions, happy little lambs carrying flame throwers, prancing innocently through sunny pastures wearing parsley hats on their heads before immolating in nuclear explosions. My sinuses opened so far I thought my brains would drop out.

I could hear Lloyd making little mewling 'oo-oo-ooo' noises from across the table, and I could hear the restaurant staff whooping and laughing with glee. The chef was bent over double, squealing like a Christmas pig, and the waiter was wiping his eyes on another diner's napkin. From somewhere I could hear muted applause and cheering.

Then it got *really* hot.

That curry had a strange addictive quality to it - for all I know the chef laced it with crack cocaine - but no matter how much it burned and made us cry like little girls, we couldn't tear ourselves away. It was the strangest culinary combination of joy and pain I've ever experienced. It was like meeting Helen of Troy, hearing her say she only had eyes for you, then having her punch you in the mouth with brass knuckles before telling you again how much she loved you. It was masochism and mastication rolled into one. My love affair with spicy food had attained full bloom.

When Lloyd and I finally finished our meals, paid our tab and got up to go back to our hotel, the staff treated us like beloved family members, shaking our hands, slapping our backs and crushing us in enthusiastic hugs. We staggered out onto the sidewalk and made our way home.

THE ONLY MAJOR DOWNSIDE TO EATING SPICY FOOD IS, WELL, SHALL WE SAY - the fallout - after the fact. An immutable universal gastric law states that what goes in must eventually come out - much to the chagrin and discomfort of the spicy food addict. It was about a two mile walk to our hotel, and we passed the time chatting about the incredible near-death experience we'd just had. As we got closer to the hotel, I noticed Lloyd had become slightly less talkative, and had increased his pace slightly. I tried to engage him in more conversation, but he ignored me as his face took on a distinctly uncomfortable, worried look. He stepped out even faster. I picked up my pace to keep up.

Then my lower intestine sounded red alert.

I was suddenly aware of the horrible consequence of my dinner choice, and realized why Lloyd was in such a hurry. We shared a bungalow room that had only one bathroom, and he was intent on getting there first. I walked faster, pulling slightly ahead. Lloyd sped up as well, taking the lead again. We continued speed walking past each other in determined silence as we neared the hotel, until we reached the front door and abandoned all pretense.

Lloyd elbowed me in the ribs, shoving me into the door jamb as he burst inside. I caught him in the lobby and cross checked him into a luggage cart loaded with bags, passing him on the inside and breaking into the courtyard that led to our bungalow. I took off around the pool at a full sprint, fumbling for my room key as I went. I could hear Lloyd close behind, cursing me and pleading for mercy in the same breath.

I made it home first, threw open the door and dove for the bathroom. As I locked the door, Lloyd crashed into it and collapsed outside, moaning and wailing in pain. "Let me in!" he cried. "Please!!"

"I can't!" I wailed back. "There's only one toilet, anyway!"

"I'll use the bathtub! LET ME IN!!! PLEEEASE!!"

I ignored him. I had pressing issues of my own.

———

LLOYD SOMEHOW HELD OUT UNTIL I WAS FINISHED, AND HE EVENTUALLY forgave me. When our deployment came to an end a few weeks later, we arranged to have our entire crew join us at the Indian restaurant for a going-away dinner. The staff greeted us with more hugs and back slaps, and the chef came out to personally welcome us. When we were all seated, one of the others looked at Lloyd.

"So, Lloyd," he said. "You've been here before. What's good?"

Lloyd and I exchanged a grin, and he looked to the chef. "Your special lamb curry for our entire group, my friend?"

The chef grinned back. "For our most favored guests? Of course, my friend! Of course!"

7
HEMOPHILIA

I AM NOT ONE OF THOSE PEOPLE WHO CAN'T STAND THE SIGHT OF BLOOD. This is not due to my innate cool headedness, but rather to long exposure in my childhood to the sight of *lots* of blood - most of which was my own. For as long as I can remember, my nose has been prone to spontaneous bleeding. It needs no provocation from me other than a good sneeze or deep concentration, and - *BAM* - it starts bleeding like an unfortunate extra in a B horror movie. I once developed a nosebleed in the middle of a physics final in college that elicited enough sympathy to allow me to take the exam over at a later date - which was fortunate, because until my nose decided to start bleeding like a stuck pig, I was well on my way to failing that exam.

Most of my nosebleeds would come at much more inopportune times. Because we had twelve kids and two parents in our family, we had two entire pews reserved for us at church. We always sat right in front, and my dad always sat right next to me. I think that was because I was the youngest, so I was the one who bore watching the most, and nobody was better at keeping a gimlet eye fixed on a fidgety kid than my dad. He would sit there with one eye on the priest and the other eye glaring menacingly at me, just daring me to act up.

Dad's off hand would be resting protectively (to the untrained eye) on my neck, but it wasn't there out of a sense of heartwarming fatherly tenderness. It was waiting to pinch my neck in a Vulcan death grip the instant I made any move that deviated a fraction of an inch from the approved sit-stand-kneel sit-stand-kneel Catholic Calisthenics routine.

For the non-Catholic reader, these exercises are performed in unison by the congregation throughout the service at predetermined intervals that make the most brutal exercise video look like an origami class. The point is that if you sit-stand-kneel sit-stand-kneel enough times, the burn in your legs will remind you of the burn of eternal damnation, and you'll either quit sinning immediately, or you'll collapse unconscious on the floor, which has the same effect. It's hard to sin when you're gasping for breath.

At any rate, church was not the time or place for me to be monkeying around, which made it the perfect time and place for my nose to start bleeding. My parents were firm believers in the show-me-blood rule of diagnosing kid injuries - in other words, if you weren't actively bleeding, you weren't actually hurt.

Sometimes bleeding by itself wasn't enough to convince them, but bleeding in church brought with it the spectre of public attention, so they would concede the point almost instantly, and let you go to the bathroom to get cleaned up. Otherwise, it would take a compound fracture or actual innards leaking out to warrant getting up during the service.

I preferred nosebleeds.

My brother Jethro was even more prolific at producing nosebleeds than I was. His nose would leak blood at the slightest provocation, and in a family with twelve kids and a dad who was a walking case study in anger management gone wrong, Jethro's nose was never without provocation. The great thing about Jethro's nosebleeds was that he also wore glasses, and any impact that brought on a nosebleed would also usually bring off his eyewear at the same time. The result was that Jethro would be stumbling around blind, groping for his glasses and bleeding on everything and everyone in the process.

As an adult, Jethro had a massive Newfoundland dog named Chumley who took great delight in swinging his wooly mammoth head into Jethro's beak. While Jethro fumbled for his loose glasses and bled all over himself, Chumley would steal his sandwich or knock him down and chew on his elbow for fun.

Chumley was a great dog.

In spite of (or possibly *because* of) having several bleeders in the house, my mom could not stand the sight of blood. She once passed out cold at a movie theater when one of the characters on screen cut himself while shaving. (He might have had help shaving from a mafia thug with a straight razor, and the thug may have shaved him *just* a bit too close for comfort - I can't be sure, because I wasn't there - even my parents drew the line at letting a five year old go to see *The Godfather*.)

As I was saying, my mom was a little queasy around blood. So it should come as no surprise that one day when she came home from work to find a trail of spilled plasma and platelets leading from the back door to the bathroom, ending in a pile of bandages on the counter and a sink splattered with gore, she was less than enthusiastic.

There was no ready explanation for the apparent crime scene, since the victim (me) had already driven himself to the emergency room. But that didn't make mom feel any more, ahem, sanguine about the situation. She went into panic mode and fled the scene, assuming that I had been ax-murdered and that the murderer was still lurking behind the towel cabinet.

The truth of the situation was somewhat less B-movie dramatic.

I had been working in the garage on a shelving unit for mom's pantry. She needed more shelving to hold all the cases of bean with bacon soup and powdered milk, so I volunteered to build some shelves in the hope of scoring some points and maybe gas money in the process. Mom had a chintzy little contractor style table saw that I was using to cut the shelves, but the saw was so flimsy it refused to hold still while you were feeding wood through the blade. The constant shifting and sliding made accurate cutting a happy fantasy, but more importantly it made keeping all your appendages permanently attached a real exercise in acrobatic caution and dumb luck.

I was feeding a narrow piece of lumber through the blade when I felt a jarring impact to my thumb. I knew immediately the blade had hit me, but thought that since I was wearing leather gloves, the glove had taken the brunt of the damage. My thumb didn't initially feel like it had been cut - it literally felt like I'd pounded it flat with a sledge hammer. I jerked my hand back and threw off the glove in one motion, instinctively clamping my thumb inside my closed fist. I was thinking how lucky I had been to not cut off my thumb when I looked down at the fallen glove.

The thumb of the glove was split open in a gash that went halfway down one side, across the top of the thumb and halfway down the other side.

That's amazing, I thought. *That much damage - it's a miracle I didn't get cut!*

Then I noticed a single small drop of red on the leather.

I turned my hand palm up. My thumb was still clenched tightly in my fist. I slowly opened my hand, cringing at the idea that I might accidentally fumble and drop my thumb in a pile of sawdust. As I released my fist to inspect the damage, my palm immediately filled with blood, which quickly overflowed through my fingers and down my wrist.

Oh crap, I thought, clamping my fist shut around my thumb again. *So much for miracles.*

I could have fainted and bled out right there, but luckily for me I had already spent seventeen years conditioning my queasiness into submission. Thousands of bloody noses had prepared me to handle just such an emergency with cool precision. I calmly turned off the table saw and walked into the house to get some bandages. As I walked from the back door to the bathroom, my eviscerated thumb continued to leak all over the floors.

When I got to the bathroom, I washed my hand in the sink and tore into a box of gauze with my teeth. I knocked bottles of aspirin and Pepto-Bismol everywhere in the process, and spread bloody evidence of my injury on almost every surface in the bathroom. It looked like a mafia hit had walked in on a shark attack.

After I had the digit trussed up in gauze and the bleeding slowed to a gradual ooze, I grabbed my car keys and went to the emergency room - leaving evidence of a horrific slaughter behind for Mom to find when she staggered home from a long day at work. Add to that her already well established aversion to the sight of blood, and it becomes clear why she would flee the house in a panic.

WHILE MOM DROVE IN RANDOM FRANTIC CIRCLES AROUND THE neighborhood, I arrived at the emergency room. The admitting nurse barely looked up as I walked in.

"What's the problem?" she asked in barely concealed annoyance.

"I ran my thumb through a table saw," I said, flourishing my bloody gauze-encased extremity.

"Not your best move, I'd say," she said. "Insurance?"

"Yeah."

She huffed. "I mean, who's your insurance provider?"

"I dunno," I said. "I'm on my mom's policy."

"You don't know the provider's name?"

"Did you know your parents' insurance company when you were seventeen?"

She glared at me. "Don't be smart. You're a minor. We can't treat you unless your guardian is present - with insurance."

"So it'd be better for me to bleed to death right here than have somebody stitch up my thumb? Yeah, I can see how that would be less risky for you. Not such a stellar plan for me, though."

"If you were accompanied by a parent, it would be no problem. I suggest you go see your general practitioner."

"Wait a minute. This *is* an emergency room, right? What do you do here if you don't treat emergencies?"

"We *do* treat emergencies," she said. "We *don't* treat unaccompanied minors whose lives are not in immediate peril."

"So you want me to drive all the way back across town, make an appointment with our family doctor, and somehow avoid crashing my car on the way after I die or pass out from blood loss? Don't you think it would be more perilous to my life for me to drive around town like this?" I waved my bloody thumb at her.

"If you're losing that much blood," she said, glaring at me over the top of her glasses, "then you should probably quit wasting time here. Off you go." She looked back at her paperwork.

I stared at her for a moment, but it was obvious she'd already forgotten that I'd ever come in. I turned and shuffled back out to my car, holding my injured thumb out in front of me. *What the hell just happened?*

MEANWHILE, MY MOM HAD CALLED OR SHOWED UP AT ALL OF MY brothers' houses, partly searching for me and partly suspecting that one of them was the ax-murderer. None of them knew what she was talking about. My brother Inigo, who is a firefighter, tried to downplay mom's worst fears.

"He's probably not dead," Inigo told her. "He's probably at the emergency room already. He'll call when he gets patched up."

"How would he know to go to the emergency room?" mom asked. "He's only been to the doctor once in his life, and that was only 'cuz he was being born at the time."

"He's dumb, but he's not completely stupid," Inigo said. "If he's not passed out in a ditch, he probably made it to the ER."

"You're not making this any better."

"Sure I am," Inigo said. "If he's in a ditch already, he can't get in a crash and hurt anybody else, and the cops are bound to find him sooner or later. If he's not in a ditch, he's at the ER, annoying the nurses but getting help anyway. Either way, it's no big deal. I'm being optimistic."

"You're being morbid. What if he was attacked and kidnapped?"

"Who would want him?"

"There's a lot of sickos out there, you know."

"Not *that* sick. Besides, what self-respecting kidnapper would take

MP, and then steal his pile of junk car, too? It makes no sense. He probably cut himself trying to open a can of bean with bacon soup, then decided to drive himself to the hospital. Or, he cut himself, bandaged it up, and went to a friend's house to watch cartoons and didn't bother to clean up his mess. That actually makes more sense. He's always been a slob."

———

BY THE TIME I DROVE BACK ACROSS TOWN TO OUR FAMILY DOCTOR'S OFFICE, I was thoroughly annoyed, and actually starting to feel a little light-headed. Luckily for me, our doctor was in the office and happened to have an opening at the moment I walked in. He gave me two painful shots to deaden the pain, then set to stitching me up. I watched in fascination as he sewed the tip of my thumb back in place. He glanced up at me.

"You feelin' queasy at all?"

"Nope," I said. "I figured I may never get a chance to watch this sort of thing again, so I'd better watch now."

"Good point," he said as he tied off the stitches. "You're all set. Try not to use your thumb for a push block next time you're using a table saw."

"Thanks, doc. I'll try to remember that."

———

I DROVE MYSELF HOME, FINDING THE HOUSE EMPTY. *BETTER CLEAN THIS mess*, I thought. *Mom would freak out if she saw it.* I cleaned everything up and settled down on the couch to watch Gilligan's Island reruns. Just then my mom burst through the door.

"MP!! WHAT IN THE WORLD?!?!??"

I looked up. "What?"

"I came home and found the house looking like a multiple murder scene! What did you do?!?!?"

I held up my thumb, neatly wrapped in a gauze ball the size of an apple. Mom recoiled.

"Did you cut it off?"

"Nah," I said. "Seven stitches. Just chopped the tip partway off, but the doc sewed it back. I didn't even hit the bone. Doc said I'll probably lose some feeling in the tip of my thumb, but otherwise it's fine."

Assured that I wasn't a newly minted amputee, mom switched instantly to practicality mode.

"How much?"

"Just about a quarter inch, is all."

"Not your silly thumb," she huffed. "How much is this gonna cost me?"

"Thanks for caring," I said. "They kicked me outta the ER, 'cuz I didn't have a parent with me. So I had to drive to our doctor's office and have him sew it up."

"That's not what I asked," she said, glaring. "How much?"

"I dunno," I said, smiling. "They said they'd bill you. But it'll probably be more than it would have cost you to have a professional build your pantry shelves."

"Smart aleck. Don't bleed on the couch. I'm gonna make some dinner. You want something?"

"Sure," I said. "How about some tomato soup?"

Mom went pale. "You're on your own. I need to go lie down."

"Can I have a glass of cranberry juice?"

She groaned.

"French fries with lots of ketchup?"

"Stop it! You're making me sick!"

"How come I'm the one who's critically injured, but you're the one who needs to lie down?"

"You don't look so hurt to me," she said. "But if you keep waving that thumb at me and talking about blood, I'm gonna pass out and you'll have to drive *me* to the ER."

"Waste of time. If I show up with an unconscious parent, they'll probably kick me out again. You'd be better off running *your* thumb through the table saw."

"Aaghhh! Stop!" She retreated to her bedroom and slammed the door.

I made my own dinner that night, and Mom didn't bother to join me. As I sliced a piece of ham for a meat sandwich, I toyed with the idea of telling her I'd cut my other thumb off with the butcher knife.

Then I thought better of it. Sometimes, squeamishness trumps humor, and even the most warped sense of humor can show a little mercy.

8

BUMPUS CULTURE

In the classic 1983 holiday movie *A Christmas Story*, Ralphie's dad is antagonized by (among a variety of other things) his hillbilly neighbors, the Bumpuses. They own a pack of incorrigible hound dogs who regularly attack his dad when he comes home from work. They also break into his kitchen on Christmas morning and devour the Christmas turkey, forcing Ralphie and his family to eat Peking Duck for Christmas dinner at a Chinese restaurant in town. Ralphie's dad refers to the dogs' owners as "Sonsabitchin'... BUMPUSES!!!"

This sentiment is shared by many people who have Bumpuses for neighbors. We've all had 'em - folks who have three wrecked cars up on blocks in their front yard, wheels missing and windows broken out. Or the ones who aspire to be race car drivers, but for some unknown reason can only test their race cars' engines between the hours of 11:30 at night and 2:30 in the morning. Or they might be the type who like to step out on their front porch in their underwear so they can scratch themselves just as your new friends from church arrive for dinner.

Every neighborhood has its Bumpus.

Bumpuses aren't always necessarily bad - some of them are salt-of-the-earth types who would give you the shirt off their back - as long as you don't mind a shirt stained with ketchup, sweat and beer. The common thread in Bumpus culture is behavior that would be frowned upon by polite society, homeowner's associations, or anyone with a weak stomach or tender sensibilities.

My brother Rico used to live across the street from a family of Bumpuses who were very friendly, polite and hard working. They were just friendly, polite and hard working while they were loud and obnoxious on the side. They liked to build race cars in their spare time, a hobby they financed by running a fleet of logging trucks from their front yard. When they got bored with revving their race car engines at all hours of the day and night, they'd switch to starting six of the logging trucks and letting them idle in the yard all day, or they'd break out their arc welder at midnight, the pulsing glow from the arc lighting up the neighborhood like the sun was going super nova.

In spite of all that, Rico couldn't help but like them. Mr. Bumpus never failed to walk across the street to chat when Rico was working in his yard, and he always offered his spare can of beer to Rico. Mr. Bumpus never walked anywhere without two cans of beer - one in his fist and one in his shirt pocket. Mathematicians carry pocket protectors - Bumpuses carry pocket beer.

My wife and I once lived in a townhouse where our neighbors' master bedroom shared a wall with ours. The people next door were proof that Bumpuses are not limited to living in the boondocks - they live and thrive in crowded cities, too. These particular Bumpuses had a nasty habit of having screaming matches and waking the entire complex at all hours of the night, starting with my wife and me. Mrs. Bumpus especially liked to stand at her bedroom window and shriek at Mr. Bumpus as he fumbled with his car keys in their driveway below, trying desperately to flee.

On several occasions they would both leave, and neither of them would bother to turn off the TV in their bedroom. The last straw for me came at around three o'clock one such morning. The Bumpuses had gone out and left *The Lord of the Rings* playing at full volume. As

Gandalf shouted defiance at the Balrog deep in the Mines of Moria, I lay in bed on the other side of the wall, staring at the ceiling and grinding my teeth.

"YOU SHALL NOT PASS!!" Gandalf shouted.

More like 'I shall not sleep', I thought. *Just hurry up and kill that ugly sucker, wizard. I have to go to work in an hour.*

Several weeks later we moved out. We were five months into a one year lease, but the penalty for moving out early was a small price to pay for getting away from Bumpus neighbors. As I loaded the moving truck in our driveway, the muffled shouting from next door tailed off and Mrs. Bumpus stepped out on her porch.

"Betcha yer glad to get away from us, right?" she asked in a sarcastic tone.

There's the understatement of the century, I thought. "Oh no," I lied, smiling at her. "We just got a good deal on a house that we couldn't pass up."

"Uh-huh. Where did you I SAID SHUT UP!!! I'M TALKING HERE!!" Her head had swiveled so fast to look and shout over her shoulder it had been a blur. She turned slowly back to face me, a thin smile plastered over her suddenly infuriated glare. "As I was saying," she said, her voice low and menacing. "Where did you say your new house is, exactly?"

"North of here," I said without a pause. "About an hour north." I smiled back. She glared at me for a long moment, then turned and went back inside. The shouting match picked up as soon as the door closed.

We moved south of there to a nice house in a new development in suburbia. We were overjoyed - surely there would be no Bumpuses living in brand new suburban housing, right?

Wrong.

A FEW MONTHS AFTER WE MOVED IN, A NEW BUMPUS COUPLE FOUND US and bought the house right behind ours. They promptly hired a contractor to attach a massive deck to the back of their house, large enough to park several helicopters on. Since their home was on a hill behind ours, the deck was at about the same level as our second floor. Every time they came out on the deck, we could see everything they did clearly from our family room window, whether we wanted to see it or not.

This Bumpus couple's claim to Bumpushood was further cemented by their elderly live-in mothers, whom we semi-affectionately referred to as The Grannies. They had several little rat dogs who liked to bark themselves hoarse anytime we dared to use our own back yard, and they didn't care to listen to anyone who told them to shut up. The Grannies spent a large portion of every day standing on their gargantuan deck, wearing mu'u mu'us and house slippers and screaming at the dogs, while the dogs studiously ignored them and barked like hairy little demons at everything that moved.

"BAAAYYYY-BEEEEEE!!!!" Grannie number one would scream in a voice that would peel paint. (The Grannies were indistinguishable from one another - they looked more like identical twins than in-laws, and since they *were* Bumpuses, being identical twins and in-laws at the same time was not outside the realm of possibilities.)

"BAAAYYYY-BEEEEEE!!!!" Grannie number two would scream, standing on the edge of the deck and stomping her foot at one of the dogs, who barked and slobbered at a squirrel on the fence. The squirrel ignored the dog, instead staring at The Grannies in horrified disbelief.

The Grannies would stand there screaming at the dog and each other for half an hour before they got hoarse and retreated inside. The dog would never notice them and would stay outside, barking furiously at everything and nothing.

My wife and I would watch or listen to these proceedings every morning, noon and night. I developed a nasty habit of grinding my teeth as a result, and my wife now has a visceral fear of mu'u mu'us (which is actually a good thing - thanks for that, Bumpus Grannies).

The couple who actually owned the house were both very overweight, and both disproportionately immodest about their physiques. Grannie number one's son Darryl was not only the size of the average silverback mountain gorilla, but he had roughly the same amount and color of hair on his body. This became obvious anytime he came outside, since Darryl never bothered to wear a shirt.

This behavior was upsetting enough when Darryl installed a massive outdoor kitchen on his deck (a shirtless silverback gorilla flipping burgers and sucking cheap beer from a can is *not* wholesome family entertainment - I don't care what kind of family you were raised in), but it became unbearable when Darryl upped the ante and installed a hot tub. This action coaxed Darryl's wife Beulah outside long enough for us to determine that she looked just like a *hairless* silverback - if hairless silverbacks wore one-piece, dangerously low-cut swimsuits in large, loud floral patterns.

One evening, I happened to glance out our kitchen window after I had filled my dinner plate with my wife's latest delicious meal. As I sadly dumped the food down the garbage disposal, my wife called to me from the dining room.

"You looked out the window, didn't you?"

"It was an accident," I pleaded. "I saw a squirrel fall backward off the fence and I wondered what killed him."

"The Bumpuses barbecuing or hot-tubbing killed him - that'd be my guess."

"Hot-tubbing," I said. "They're playing Marco Polo again."

"Ughh," my wife said. "Now I've lost my appetite, too." Watching the Bumpuses play Marco Polo in their hot tub would have been a good diet plan, if it weren't for the violent nausea it caused as a side effect.

ANOTHER ANNOYING THING ABOUT BUMPUSES IS THEIR INNATE ABILITY TO avoid the consequences of their behavior. They're mostly impervious to regulation, prosecution or harsh criticism. I discovered this baffling trait one summer afternoon when I was opening my mail. One envelope contained a nastygram from our homeowner's association, notifying me that they had spotted a weed in my front flowerbed. The

Homeowner's Association wanted the weed removed immediately, if not sooner, or they promised they would do something unspeakable to my credit rating. Since the president of the HOA was a friend of mine, I called him on the phone.

"Hey," I said when he picked up, "what's the big idea, threatening to put a lien on my house because of one dandelion? Don't you think that's a bit extreme?"

"Not really," he said. "That's what you pay dues for."

"I pay dues so you can threaten me? That makes no sense."

"Sure it does," he said. "We can't afford to have the place start looking run down, can we?

"I dunno," I said. "Have you seen the Bumpuses back yard lately? They have blackberry bushes pushing my back fence down, their dog pack is about a dozen strong, and the gazebo over their hot tub is listing about twenty degrees to starboard. Did you send them a nastygram too?"

"Nope. They ignore our nastygrams. We don't bother sending them anymore."

"Did you put a lien on their house?"

"Nah," he said. "Wouldn't do any good. They quit making house payments two years ago."

"So lemme get this straight," I said. "You send me a nastygram threatening to destroy my credit over a six-inch dandelion, because you know I'm responsible and I'll go out and pull it - but you let the Bumpuses keep a pack of wild dogs in their back jungle, because you know they don't care what you say to them?"

"Yeah, that sounds about right."

"Good talk," I said, hanging up the phone.

"Were you nice?" My wife asked.

"Of course I was nice," I said. "Fat lot of good it did me, though."

"Did they threaten the Bumpuses, too?"

"No. But he said that if we start wearing mu'u mu'us and breeding wolves, the HOA will make an exception for our dandelion."

"Did you tell him about their gazebo leaning to one side? I swear that thing is gonna fall over and kill somebody."

"I told him," I said. "But I'm not so sure we want them to do anything about that. If it does fall over, it might get a couple of dogs and at least one Bumpus. Be an improvement."

"We're not that lucky," she said. "So what're you gonna do?"

"I'm going out front to pull that dandelion," I said, pulling off my shirt. "Do we have any canned beer?"

9
STUDEBAKER SLEDDING

MODERN DAY VEHICLES, LIKE MODERN DAY DIAPERS, ARE MOSTLY disposable.

This has not always been the case. I grew up in a not too-bygone era in which cars were made to last - no matter how much abuse they got at the hands of their drivers. Cars of the good-ol-days vintage were tough, because teenaged drivers of the good-ol-days were mostly twits.

My first car was, like most of the other necessities of life for the youngest of twelve kids, a hand-me-down. My grandparents had purchased it new several years before I had been born new, and many years later when my grandmother became too unpredictable to drive, the car was relegated to teenager transportation duty.

It was a 1963 Studebaker Lark four-door sedan. The original color had been something in the maroon family optimistically dubbed 'Rose Mist', but because my grandparents were products of difficult lives that demanded no waste and even less frivolity, the car had never been waxed and the paint had subsequently faded to something approximating dried-out Pepto-Bismol. We affectionately referred to it as 'The Rude-i-Quaker', 'The Rutabaga', or more simply, 'The Stoody' or 'The Rudy'.

It was a hideous thing, but I loved it.

No other kid in my high school had anything like it. That probably had something to do with the fact that no other kid in my high school would have been caught dead driving anything like it. Teen angst and self-loathing is bad enough, without adding four-wheeled humiliation to your plate everywhere you go. Fortunately, my humiliation-filled upbringing made me immune to such silliness, and I saw The Rudy as a blessing in a very ugly disguise. It was freedom with a steering wheel, carbureted liberty powered by a small block V8 engine.

The Rudy had a trunk big enough to hide a body in, and the back seat had room for a singles tennis match. There were no seat belts, no air conditioning, no FM radio, no cruise control, and no power steering, power brakes or power windows. The sickeningly pink paint was rotted through in several places low on the body, where road grime and moisture had taken hold over the years. The tires were discount store retreads that looked like they would turn into whoopee cushions at the slightest stress, and the upholstery was covered by surplus Army blankets that could have doubled as emergency sandpaper.

The good point of the car was that it always started - every time. It didn't matter if it was twenty below zero outside and the car was frozen in a ten foot high snow drift; if it had gas in the tank, it would always start when you needed it to. The heater was strong enough to power a Turkish bath house, and the engine strong enough to give me my first experience of speed in excess of 100 miles per hour.

It was a teenage boy's dream.

I DROVE THE RUDY EVERYWHERE. TO SCHOOL, WORK, DUCK HUNTING, camping - you name it. Wealthy friends of mine enjoyed fancy new four wheel drive trucks paid for by their indulgent parents, but I didn't let potential vehicular embarrassment keep me from having fun. The Rudy could go anyplace those guys could go - almost. I hardly ever passed up an opportunity to test the Rudy's off-road abilities. I'd happily forge ahead on impassable-looking roads until I could forge no farther, then I'd slap the Rudy in reverse and smoke the bologna-skin tires until I got out.

On one trip, however, reverse wasn't enough to fix the predicament I'd driven into. I was with my buddies Waylon, Duke and Cheeb, and we were planning to drive to a mountain lake and catch the first fish of the spring. Problem was, my three friends (who all had access to four-wheel-drives) were low on gas money, which left The Rudy as the only viable transport.

It was early April, so most of the forest roads were still covered in snow. Add four strapping young men to an old sedan with a doughy suspension, and the Rudy's already minimal ground clearance sagged to almost nil. As we rounded a bend in the dirt road and were confronted by a large snowdrift blocking our path, I realized we might not make it to the lake.

"Whatcha stopping for?" Duke asked me.

"I'm, uh, just thinking," I said. "I don't know if The Rudy can make it through that with all of us inside. We're bottoming out the shocks already."

"C'mon, punch it!!" Cheeb shouted from the back seat. "I wanna go fishin'!"

I shot a glance at Waylon. He was the most normal of the three, and was sometimes the voice of reason. He just grinned back at me. No help there.

"O-K," I said. "Watch this!"

I shifted The Rudy into reverse and backed around the corner. Then I revved the engine a couple of times for effect, dropped the transmission into gear, and stomped on the gas. We came around the bend in the road, fishtailing slightly as we accelerated toward the drift. Duke and Cheeb were whooping and hollering from the back seat, and Waylon had a large grin on his face. We closed on the snow drift at an alarming speed, and I cringed a little just before impact.

But instead of coming to an abrupt stop and throwing me through the windshield to my death, The Rudy nosed its way to the top of the drift, getting up on step like a drug runner's jet boat with the Coast Guard hot on its tail. The gentle fishtailing became a graceful slalom across the virgin snow, and I was mesmerized by how suddenly smooth the ride was. It was like The Rudy had turned into a hydrofoil, and we were riding on a perfectly smooth cushion of air. I spun the wheel gently back and forth depending on the direction of the slide, keeping us more or less on course.

Then the snow drift ended and the tires made rasping contact with gravel on the other side. The soft shooshing noise of the snow was replaced by the coarse skidding of retread tires on loose gravel (not to mention the coarse language skidding from my mouth). The Rudy's grille suddenly pointed at an immense boulder on the side of the road, and my three passengers hollered for all they were worth while I frantically cranked the wheel like the captain of the Titanic. At the last moment, the nose came reluctantly around, and the boulder passed harmlessly inches off the port side, barely missing my side-view mirror.

There was a pause - a pregnant moment of silence as the others collected their thoughts and took inventory of their various parts. Then they erupted.

"YOU ALMOST KILLED US, DUDE!!" Cheeb hollered, pounding his palm on the roof above him. "THAT WAS AWESOME!!"

"DO IT AGIN, DO IT AGIN!!!" Duke shouted.

"Heh-heh," I chuckled, prying my fingers away from the steering wheel.

Waylon was grinning at me from the passenger seat. "Pretty cool," he said. "We might make it to the lake yet!"

I allowed myself a smile too. It *had* been fun, after all. The car was undamaged and nobody was bleeding, so I relaxed a bit as we rounded the next bend - and bore down on a drift twice the height and width of the first. Before the others could start cheering, I'd already mashed the accelerator to the floor. I only had a vague apprehension about what might be happening to The Rudy's undercarriage while we sledded from one drift to the next. I hadn't heard any obvious sounds of catastrophic mechanical failure, so I pressed on.

The road narrowed as it climbed and wound up the mountain toward the lake, and the frequency and size of the drifts increased exponentially. We tobogganed from one to the next, sliding nearly out of control and narrowly dodging the cliff face on one side of the road and the sheer drop on the other. We were all cackling and laughing, not a care in our teen-aged heads.

Then the car lurched to a stop.

We were suddenly stuck fender deep in a huge, broad drift that continued out of sight around the next corner. The car had stopped several feet short of the downhill edge of the road, near the center point of a 'Y' formed by the main road and a logging trail that branched off to the right and disappeared over a cliff. I put it in reverse and stood on the gas. The wheels spun around at Mach 6, melting the snow around them into a perfect slippery bowl. The back of the car started drifting slowly downhill toward the chasm at the middle of the 'Y'.

"I gotta pee," Cheeb said as he opened his door behind me and dove out.

"Me too," Duke said. He opened his door before realizing the cliff was on his side. His shriek was so high pitched it made a twelve year old girl's scream sound like the mating call of a bull moose. "AAIIAAAAIIHHHHH!!!"

Waylon was desperately trying to climb over me to get out of the car on my side. "LEMMEOUT! LEMMEOUT! LEMMEOUTTTTT!!!!"

I pushed Waylon's hand away from my eyes and slapped his knee away from my kidney. "Stop it! You're making it worse!" He stepped on my kneecap, pressing my right foot onto the gas pedal. Duke squealed from the back seat as Cheeb watched in horror from the side of the road. I managed to get my foot away from the gas long enough to shift the transmission into 'park', and the car settled into its ruts and stopped sliding. Waylon was half in my lap and half out my window. He looked down at me with a sheepish grin.

"Er, uh… sorry 'bout that," he said, shifting his elbow out of my solar plexus.

"No problem," I said. I was busy fighting back my own urge to leap out of the car. The sensation of sliding hadn't completely gone away yet, and I didn't want to be around if The Rudy slid over the cliff. I have a strong aversion to death by sudden deceleration trauma.

A soft thud came from behind us as Duke finally extricated himself from the tangled Army blanket seat cover and fell out of the back door in a heap. He popped up off the ground. "Boy, were you guys scared! You shoulda seen the looks on your faces!!"

"You should talk, Mary," Waylon said. "I think you busted my eardrums with your screaming. You sure you're a dude?"

"Yeah," Duke said, his brow furrowing. "Why?"

I looked at Cheeb, who was standing like a statue on the edge of the road, staring off in the distance. "You all right? I thought you said you had to pee."

"I think I might have already," Cheeb said. He shook his head abruptly and glared at me. "You just made the list, buddy."

"Don't make threats," I said. "I happen to know three clowns who scream like little girls and wet themselves over a little danger. That's not gonna play very well with your tough-guy images. But I might keep quiet if you help me dig this sucker out."

"Done."

"I wasn't scared," Waylon said as we gathered around The Rudy's trunk. "I was trying to rescue Cheeb."

"Nobody tried to rescue *me*," Duke pouted.

"You wouldn'ta died," I said. "You'da been the one to survive and give interviews to reporters afterward. *'I tried to save 'em but the flames were too thick. Look, I got a sliver!'*"

"Good one, dude!" Duke was easily entertained, even when the entertainment was at his own expense.

I opened the trunk. "Lemme just get the shovel..." I rummaged furiously through the jumble of junk, searching for my camping shovel. All I found was a cracked canoe paddle. I held it up. "Well, this is really gonna blow..."

I SPENT THE NEXT HOUR CARVING FOOT-SQUARE BLOCKS OF SNOW OUT OF the drift behind the car, while Cheeb and Waylon pelted Duke with snowballs. Occasionally they'd fire one in my direction, and I'd angrily swat at it, swinging the canoe paddle like a cricket bat. Finally, exhausted and soaked in sweat, I collapsed against The Rudy's rusty fender.

73

"That's as good as it's gonna get!" I gasped, throwing the canoe paddle into the depths of the trunk. Duke cocked his throwing arm back, a snowball grasped in a knuckleball grip and aimed at my head. I glared daggers at him.

"Never mind," he said, dropping his snowball. "We ready to go fishin' yet?"

"Sure," I said, tossing his fishing pole to him. "But you better start walking now if you want to get there before dark."

"Walk? Whaddya mean, walk?"

Suddenly a snowball detonated on Duke's left temple. "You forget something, man?" Cheeb was already packing another snowball. "We almost drove off the edge of the world, got buried in a snowbank, and we're still four miles from the lake. I wanna go fishin' too, but not that bad." He slung the snowball at Waylon, who caught it and threw it at Duke.

"Aww, man…" Duke whined.

Ten minutes later, with me rocking The Rudy from forward to reverse and the other guys pushing and swearing, we broke free of the snow and turned for home. The guys were disappointed at not getting to go fishing, but not getting to die in a fiery crash made up for it.

SEVERAL MONTHS LATER, I WAS ON MY WAY HOME FROM ANOTHER FRIEND'S house, happily bombing along in The Rudy. I was approaching a 'T' intersection with a busy street, so I waited until the last possible minute before engaging the brake. Remember, I *was* a teenage boy at this point, so my actions and common sense usually had very little time together. So I waited until the last minute - and instead of firmly dragging The Rudy to a full stop, the brake pedal went limp and sank all the way to the floor. My eyes popped wide open at the sight of the busy intersection ahead, and I resorted to desperate measures - I slammed the gearshift into 'park'.

The Rudy's automatic transmission seized up, the rear wheels locked, and we slid to a stop in a cloud of smoke, the front bumper two inches past the stop bar on the road. Cars whizzed by in both directions just beyond The Rudy's hood, and I started to understand how Cheeb had felt in the snowdrift. Even worse, I was certain I had killed my car.

Still rattled by my latest near-death experience, I took a deep breath and gingerly shifted into drive, looking for an opening in traffic. The oncoming cars finally parted enough to allow a battleship through with extra room for a leaky oil tanker or two on either side, so I pressed on the gas. The engine revved, but The Rudy and I were frozen in place.

RRRRRRR.....THUNK!!

The transmission suddenly kicked in, snapping the car forward and my head backward like the business end of a bobble head doll. We shot out into the intersection, and I struggled to get control of the car as it careened down the road. I knew I had done something horrible to the transmission, but luckily, my teenage brain was able to rationalize the situation as follows:

- 1. Slamming the thing into park at 45 miles per hour was probably a bad idea.
- 2. Slamming into oncoming traffic at 45 miles per hour was definitely a bad idea.
- 3. Using the emergency brake instead would have been a good idea.
- 4. By choosing the lesser of two bad ideas, I had wisely saved myself as well as countless others - and could therefore forget my neglect of the one good idea.
- 5. I was a hero.
- 6. I was a hero with a ruined transmission and no money to fix it.
- 7. After vigorous pumping on the pedal, the brakes had miraculously healed themselves.
- 8. The transmission had also miraculously healed itself, as evidenced by the fact that I was now in forward motion.
- 9. Maybe if I continued to ignore the problem, it would heal itself even more.

- 10. No one must know of this incident, because they might do something to spoil my discovery of mechanical magic - like force me to pay for repairs.

I held to this theory for the rest of the next year that I drove The Rudy, and it sort of worked. The transmission never got any better, but it never got any worse, either. Every time you'd shift from park to drive, there was a two second delay before it would actually kick into gear, threatening whiplash to unsuspecting passengers. I got used to it, because I couldn't afford to fix it. Financial desperation breeds adaptability, and driving The Rudy until it exploded couldn't possibly be much more expensive than intentionally turning it over to a mechanic before it was absolutely necessary.

And just in case you discount my theory of mechanical magic, consider this. These events took place in the early 1980s. As recently as 2010, there was a confirmed Rudy sighting in my hometown, and the car was actually in motion under its own power at the time. The Rudy survived twenty years of use before I got my hands on it, then it survived at least another two and a half decades after that - in spite of it being used as a power sled and a transmission torture test bed while I had it. The Rudy, despite being ugly and embarrassing, was virtually indestructible.

They just don't make 'em like they used to - because if they did, there'd be no market for new cars.

10

FISHING FOLLIES

SOME PEOPLE FIND IT NECESSARY TO PURSUE FISH IN EVERY CREEK, BOG, mud puddle and horse trough they pass. I am not one of these people. I don't mind eating fish; I just have no desire to spend hours trying to catch them in the wilderness. Why bother? I can pick them up with very little effort at the local deli, shrink wrapped and ready to cook. If I ever actually caught a fish in the wild, maybe my interest in the sport would increase, but I doubt it. In my view, fishing is nothing but a grand waste of time; a cover story men tell their wives when they want to avoid tedious chores or get away from the house for an uninterrupted nap.

One spring day several years ago, my brothers and I cooked up a plan to go for a day hike into the mountains. Our party consisted of two rabid fishermen (my brother Rico and our brother-in-law Rooney); and three committed non-fishermen (myself and my brothers Jethro and Inigo). Our plan was to hike in to a remote mountain lake and spend the day there in pursuit of our individual ideas of fun. Rico and Rooney were bent on thrashing the lake into a froth in pursuit of half-starved fish; Jethro wanted to climb the mountain on the far side of the lake; Inigo wanted to take a nap. I was just along for the hike.

During the drive to the trailhead, Jethro convinced me (mostly by artful use of words like 'sissy' and 'wimp') that I needed to climb the mountain with him. Brothers are persuasive like that. Inigo, a year older than Jethro and quite familiar with this ploy (having taught it to Jethro many years earlier), didn't fall for it. He was determined to take his nap. Secretly, I applauded Inigo's wisdom and wanted to take a nap too, but Jethro's continued crowing about how he was going to hike circles around me left me with no alternative. My recreation of choice would be dislodging rocks from the trail directly above Jethro's head as I hiked circles around *him*.

At the trailhead, Rooney and Rico made wagers on who would catch the first, most, and biggest fish. As I understand it, this multi-layered bet allows each fisherman several chances to snatch not only fish, but bragging rights from the chosen body of water. After agreeing on terms, Rooney reached into the back of Jethro's truck and pulled out a float tube. It had so many bells and whistles, it looked like a marching band minus the legs. He claimed that it would get him to the deep water, where all the best fish were. Rico was unimpressed. He calmly reached into the back of his own truck and produced a fully inflated two-man raft. Since Rooney's tube was still flat, Rico had a distinct head start on the deep water. Rooney started grinding his teeth.

Our trail of choice was the shortest, albeit steepest, route into the lake. After the first twenty-five yards, Rico was already having trouble carrying all of his gear. Maneuvering a fully inflated rubber raft through thick brush up the side of a mountain without dropping your fishing pole, day pack, or gallon jug of water takes a good deal of coor-dination - which Rico didn't have. Unable to stand the spectacle (or Rooney's evil snickering) any longer, I put Rico's water jug in my pack and offered to carry his fishing pole for him. This freed up both of his hands to control the raft. After some thought, he decided the best way to carry the ungainly thing was upside down on his back, much like a fur trapper portaging a canoe.

We found out later that portaging wasn't the only thing Rico could do like a fur trapper.

We trundled on up the trail, only stopping to rest every hour, or every 25 yards - whichever came first. Each stop was filled with more bragging, wagering and a good deal of wheezing and gasping. We'd all drop our gear in a heap and find a comfortable piece of rock to collapse on until we caught our breath. When our hearts had finally stopped pounding like jackhammers, we'd gather our gear and start again.

In spite of the frequent delays, Rooney and I gradually pulled away from the others. I knew that getting to the lake ahead of Jethro would give me first shot at character insults, and Rooney knew it would give him time to puff and wheeze his float tube into a state of near inflation before Rico had a chance to catch first, most, or biggest fish.

After much exertion, we dragged ourselves over the last ridge to the lakeshore. As I gazed out over the frigid blue water, I tried to decide if leaping in would be a good way to restart my heart or just put me out of my misery from the climb. Rooney wasted no time in such contemplation. He put his frantic huffing and puffing to good use by blowing up his tube.

I watched his progress, wondering what was so great about fishing. All that work, all that money spent on equipment, all that precious oxygen wasted on flotation devices. Rooney ignored me, and soon had his tube ready to go. He set it down and opened his rod case. As I watched, I vaguely remembered carrying a rod case something like that earlier in the day.

Strange.

Why would I be carrying a fishing rod? I don't fish.

Then, off in the distance, I heard the faint sounds of Rico thrashing through the brush with his raft. Suddenly, it all came rushing back.

"Uhh, Rooney… did you happen to pick up Rico's fishing rod?"

Rooney raised his head and flashed a triumphant grin, the type worn by a race car driver at the moment he realizes the guy with the fastest car forgot to fill it up with gas.

"Have a nice walk," he said, all the urgency of a moment before turning to smug confidence.

My heart sank. Rico was getting closer, and I knew his fishing rod wasn't. The fact I'm no fisherman may have contributed to my inadvertently leaving the rod leaning against a stump at our third or fourth rest stop (roughly 150 yards from the trucks and 150 miles from the lake). My mind raced, scrambling to find some excuse for the absence of the rod, desperately looking for a way to pass the buck. Suddenly Rico burst from the brush, bent over double with the raft almost scraping the ground in front of him, dripping sweat like a sumo wrestler at a fat farm.

"Tell me you picked up your rod," I said, hoping maybe he had it hidden from view somewhere. He peered out at me from under the raft, a blank look on his face. Then the horrible truth hit him: he had spent three hours huffing and puffing up the side of a mountain with a rubber raft on his back for nothing. Even worse, Rooney was going to win the bet without even trying.

What followed was a spirited demonstration of Rico's other fur trapper ability – swearing a blue streak so wide and long, any fur bearing animal within 20 miles would have happily shed its skin in order to lighten up and make a quick getaway. He flung the raft to the ground in disgust, trying to straighten his spine so he could kill me from an upright position. I decided I urgently needed to be someplace else, before he could find a handy blunt object. I knew the only way to make amends was to reunite him with his fishing rod as soon as possible; ideally before Rooney caught any fish. I bolted.

About fifty yards from the lake, I passed Inigo and Jethro, both strolling along contentedly. "What's with you?" Jethro asked the back of my head as I shot by.

"Left Rico's rod against a stump. Gotta get it!!" Jethro's howling laughter only spurred me on as I dropped over the edge of the ridge.

Instead of following the trail and wasting time zig-zagging through a hundred switchbacks, I opted for the direct approach: Aim straight downhill and pray you don't hit anything sharp. Or hungry. Or sharp *and* hungry. I vaulted a log and sailed off into unknown territory.

THE GROUND OFF THE TRAIL WAS UNDER ABOUT A FOOT OF SNOW, WHICH was not quite hard enough to bear my weight. I knew the snow concealed a collection of items hazardous to my health - rocks, branches, badger holes, hibernating bears - but I had no choice. I leapt over huge clumps of buck brush, ducked under overhanging tree limbs, and dodged through impenetrable thickets without breaking stride. I ignored the vicious slapping of low hanging branches around my face and shoulders, knowing the slapping Rico had in mind would be much worse.

After twenty minutes of bushwhacking, I shot out of the trees onto the trail. Miraculously, I was only ten feet uphill from Rico's fishing pole, which was leaning undisturbed exactly where I had left it. I snatched it up and started back to the lake. The return trip, scrambling up the almost vertical trail as fast as I could go, took at least five years off my life. I didn't mind the loss much, since five years was small potatoes compared to how short Rico would want to cut my life if he lost any part of the bet to Rooney.

WHEN I FINALLY STAGGERED BACK OVER THE LAST RIDGE, ROONEY WAS rummaging through his tackle box with an extremely peevish look on his face. Inigo was sitting against a tree nearby, snoozing away the day. Jethro was hitting rocks into the lake with a large stick, ignoring Rooney's threats of bodily harm for scaring away the fish. Surprisingly, Rico was not waiting for me with a club and homicidal intent. He was sitting on a stump at the water's edge, looking sullen.

I wobbled up behind him, wheezing apologies as I held out his fishing pole in my quivering hand. I braced myself, expecting him to separate my spleen from the rest of me with a raft paddle. Instead, he looked up and blurted out, "I'm a bad brother!" he wailed. "I'm sorry!"

"Huh?" I squeaked. I was either hallucinating, or delirious, or both.

Jethro interrupted his batting practice to explain. "After you ran away like a little girl," he said, "Rico cut loose with an epic hissy fit. He was kicking rocks, stomping up and down, and making all kinds of plans to murder you."

"Yeah," Inigo said, opening one eye. "We saved your life."

"Wait, what?"

"Yup," Jethro went on, letting out a deep, smug sigh. "If we hadn't shamed him so bad, he might have actually killed you. Lucky for you we were here."

"I'll be happy to kill all of you idiots," Rooney growled, his face buried deep in his tackle box, "if you don't SHADDAP AND QUIT SCARING ALL THE FISH!" He suddenly jumped up and threw the tackle box against a tree.

"What's with him?" I asked, forgetting all about Rico.

Inigo stretched his arms and let out a satisfied yawn. "Rooney's just mad 'cuz he spent the first half hour after you left teasing Rico about how he was gonna lose the bet."

"Which made Rico even madder," Jethro added. He looked sideways at Rico. "Where'd you even learn some of that cussin', anyway?"

"From Dad," Rico muttered, shuffling his toe in the dirt.

"Cusser mouth," Inigo said.

"I said I was sorry!" Rico whined.

"Cork it, both of ya," Jethro snapped. "As I was saying, Rico had a hissy fit, and Rooney made it worse." We all looked at Rooney, who was angrily kicking his float tube while trying to untangle a ball of fishing line from around one arm. He ignored us. "So Rooney was gloating about how bad he was gonna beat Rico," Jethro continued. "But then his float tube started leaking like a cheap diaper, and he almost drowned! HAR!"

"I said, SHADDAP!" Now the end of Rooney's rod was tangled in the branches of a tree. "SON OF A..."

"Don't mind him," Inigo said. "He's a sore loser."

"I ain't lost ANYTHING yet!" Rooney shouted.

"Anyway," Jethro said, glaring at Inigo, "Rooney was gloating until his float tube pulled a *Titanic* on him. It's hard to brag when you're going 'blub', so while he was going down for the third time, me and Inigo ganged up on Rico here. Told him he oughta be ashamed, making you run back down the mountain like that."

"Yeah, ya big meany," Inigo offered.

"I'M SORRY!" Rico wailed.

"GAAAGGH!" Rooney screamed at the tree.

"Shaddap, the three of ya," Jethro said. "So after Rico cussed for a while…"

"Yeah, *Dad*," Inigo said.

"I'm NOT DAD!" Rico said. "I said I was sorry, dangit!"

"Will you clowns ALL SHADDAP so ONE of you can tell me what happened?" I demanded. Jethro smirked. Rico pouted. Rooney threw his rod in the lake.

"It's like this," Inigo said. "Rico cussed a blue streak while Rooney launched his float tube. Then Rooney's float tube went submarine on him, and me and Jethro humiliated Rico. Rico's guilty conscience got the better of him, and he started feeling bad about chasing you after his rod."

"Yeah, 'cuz you don't even like to fish," Jethro said.

"Ya think?" I said, glaring at Jethro.

"So the rest of the time you were gone," Inigo continued, "Rooney tried fishing from the bank. He lost all his fancy lures on submerged logs, and never even got a nibble! He not only didn't catch first, biggest or most fish - he didn't catch ANY FISH! What a dope!"

Rooney popped an antacid tablet into his mouth, but said nothing.

Rico looked at me. "I'm sorry, MP," he said. "I'm a bad brother! I wasn't really gonna kill ya! You can break my fishing pole if you want! Rooney just ticked me off is all."

"He has that effect on people," I said. "Don't sweat it."

His remorse suddenly evaporated. "Can I have my rod back, then?"

"Er, yeah. No problem." He snatched it from me, vaulted into his raft, and started fishing with vigor.

"Ain't no fish in this stupid lake, anyway," Rooney muttered, walking away from the water's edge in disgust. Just as I turned to follow him, we heard a triumphant shout from the middle of the lake.

"Rooo-neeey! Looky what I got!!!!"

Rooney acted like he'd been stuck with a hot poker. "AAIIGGHH!!!"

I think that's fisherman lingo for conceding defeat in a bet.

THE NEXT HALF HOUR OR SO SAW RICO REELING IN FISH OF ALL SHAPES AND sizes, each new catch announced by a happy "Rooo-neeeey..." and greeted by another pained response, most of which are unsuitable for print.

Rico went on to claim victory in the categories of first, biggest, and most fish, all of which could have been accomplished with just one fish, since Rooney didn't catch anything at all. Rico attributed his success to ingenuity and earthworms: Apparently, fish who have spent an entire winter frozen in the ice of a mountain lake like a fish stick in a freezer case are much more interested in raw meat than artificial lures.

Rooney, taking the high tech approach, had shunned earthworms as "poor man's bait", opting instead to use all varieties of artificial lures - which were no more appealing to a starving fish than a hubcap from a 1963 Studebaker. He not only lost the bet, but was forced to put up with ridicule from the rest of us for having squandered an unbelievably long head start.

JETHRO HAD DELAYED CLIMBING THE MOUNTAIN ON THE FAR SIDE OF THE lake in my absence, but after Rico caught his first fish, he was itching to go. "So – you done stalling? Ready for a real hike?"

I answered with silence and a murderous look, and Jethro decided the prudent thing to do was to keep his insults to himself and go it alone. He later regaled us with tales of wading through knee-deep snow and navigating trackless wilderness on his way to the summit. I was unimpressed. Finding one's way to the top of a small mountain in the forest requires nothing more than the ability to figure out which way is up. Running downhill through a jungle under threat of imminent death and coming out within yards of a lost fishing pole is like finding a needle in a haystack with a gun to your head.

Inigo whiled away the rest of the day lying in the sun with his hat pulled down over his eyes, enjoying the peaceful, uninterrupted sleep that only a man avoiding enforced yard work can truly appreciate. After the commotion over the fishing bet died down, I took my cue from him and settled in to enjoy a nap of my own. Sleep came easily after my ordeal, but I kept one eye cracked open and aimed at Rooney, just in case he tried to take out his frustrations on me. After all, I had effectively armed Rico with the instrument of Rooney's destruction. Luckily for me he wasn't in a vengeful mood, and he spent the rest of the day grumbling about worms and "stupid fish."

To Rico's credit, he has never changed his account of the expedition to shine a more favorable light on himself. To this day, mere mention of the trip causes him to wail in despair and beg me for forgiveness. A lesser (fisher)man might try to justify his behavior as acceptable simply because it was fishing season, and a bet is a bet. But in Rico's case, blood is still thicker than water - even when that water is full of starving fish, and he's got the only effective bait for miles around.

ABOUT THE AUTHOR

M.P. MacDougall is an American historian and author of thrillers, humorous satire and fantasy. The youngest of twelve children, he grew up on a suburban farm, spending much of his free time chasing cows, perfecting bicycle stunts and playing in the dirt, and he never had to wear a helmet or use anti-bacterial soap. He was a professional Air Traffic Controller for more than twenty-six years, and a practitioner of the art of sarcastic banter and snide commentary for much longer than that. He holds a Bachelor of Arts in World Military History, because he's afraid he'll lose it if he puts it down. He lives with his very patient wife and kids in the Pacific Northwest of the United States.

ALSO BY M.P. MACDOUGALL

Lawson Holland Thrillers

One Is A Warrior- FREE Novella download at MPMacDougall.com

The Blood of Tyrants

The Blood of Patriots

The Tree of Liberty

Sing Your Death Song

How To Steer Your Kid Series (Humor/Satire)

Jet Screamer

Meat Sandwiches

Harvey Bennett Prequels (With Nick Thacker)

The Icarus Effect

Learn more about the author at MPMacDougall.com

Thanks so much for reading!

www.ingramcontent.com/pod-product-compliance
Lightning Source LLC
Chambersburg PA
CBHW022045170626
46808CB00003B/1373